Curiosity Killed the Elf

I. N. KNIGHT

For FeralM4ves for being the first fan of Allonwë and Natanael.
This book would not exist without you. They would not exist without you. Thank you for bringing me joy to create this silly little book.

NEVER TRUST INANIMATE OBJECTS

"A princess," the voice began, scrambling the monks in the library who knew the tone all too well.

"Who meets a prince-"

A loud crash followed the words for emphasis on each pause.

"Falls madly in love with him-"

More crashing.

"-Gets hitched to said prince, then lives happily ever after-"

Pause for dramatic effect.

"Has got to be one of the most gag-inducing stories ever conceived! Where's the chaos? Where's the intrigue? What? No adventure for her, too? Neither has to work to fall in love? They just spot each other and immediately decide to procreate?"

The angry grumbling amongst the library shelves had only grown more raucous before someone had alerted the proper authorities, but it persisted.

"And why does the princess have to fall madly in love with the prince?" the ranter continued. "Can't he fall in love with her and follow her around like a love-sick puppy first? And does it even have to be a prince? Why not some random person off the street?"

The monks attempted to restore calm in the library, but each time a discarded romance novel was thrown at them. There was a crash and a flutter of paper as another hit a decorative piece on the mantle over the fireplace, shattering it. The sound of heavy boots alongside some much softer scuffling shoes and muted, frantic muttering making its way down the corridor signaled help was arriving soon.

"And why must it be 'madly'? Wouldn't it be more prudent to fall 'happily' in love with someone? If you were mad at each other all the time, why on earth would you skip to saying your wedding vows? I mean, how long is that going to last-"

"Princess," Natanael said flatly, interrupting her rant. The only one brave enough to, judging by the fact the area had been deserted around them. "Perhaps it's time for a new subject."

Allonwë, the ranting princess in question, looked over at her personal bodyguard, blinking out of her swirling thoughts and back to the present. He'd snatched the book out of her hand mid throw and nearly put her off balance. He had probably been 'beseeched to quell the tumultuous princess' again.

She frowned, but not at him. He was always the one they called when no one else could get through to her. He'd been at a meeting of the guards that morning, which is why she'd gone off on her own into the library to entertain herself, only to end up like this.

Natanael had been her bodyguard since he'd become of age nearly half a century ago, not that he looked any older than his early twenties by human standards. Elves didn't show age in their face, they showed it in their ears. The longer an elf's ears were, the older they were. Which opened up rude comments about elf ears in general like 'knife ears' or for the really, really old ones, 'rope ears'. Elves couldn't die by natural causes, but many things could kill them. So, by many standards, she and Natanael were still very young elves.

They'd grown up together, but Natanael was overprotective, much more overprotective of her than he should have been. That was her parents' great and terrible idea. Can't have the princess skipping about and having fun! Then again, her redheaded temper and insatiable curiosity that got them both into difficult situations might have convinced her parents her version of fun was a tad... chaotic, and therefore not 'proper' for a princess.

Maybe. They could just hate fun, Allonwë had decided.

Few people ever saw her wild side, legendary though it was. Tales of Allonwë's misadventures were well known throughout Sitani castle. However, she unfortunately always got caught in the aftermath because only Allonwë would or could ever pull off something so ridiculous. Natanael was an exception to that privilege, though, as he was usually along for the ride (to curb her actions to less than disastrous). Most of the time, he was the only one that could. Though when he couldn't, it was usually ridiculously beyond anyone's control.

Which was why, when she'd begun hurling books and ranting about romance novels, they had summoned Natanael to calm her.

"Don't they have anything interesting in this place?" she complained. "It's like if you've read one book around here, you've read them all unless you count the philosophy section where everyone rambles about meaningless things and makes them complicated!"

"Perhaps try something besides reading, princess," Natanael suggested, rubbing the bridge of his nose.

She'd probably interrupted his meeting for this, she realized. Regardless, it brought him back to her so she wouldn't be as bored. Natanael had been her closest friend and confidant, on top of being her personal bodyguard, and she trusted him like no one else. She also took advantage of him

3

like no one else. And he let her. There was a soft spot there for her and Allonwë tapped into that as much as he would allow her.

"Like what?" she asked, hoping to get him to prompt an idea she could build from and make interesting. It was a talent of hers that she'd honed lately, and Natanael was struggling to stay ahead of it.

"Perhaps a game," he replied, then winced. If he suggested something which she took to her own meaning and got in trouble, it would be his fault. "Of chess!" He swiftly added, though the light had already kindled within Allonwë's eyes.

"Oh, a game!" she exclaimed. "I quite like the idea of that!"

"I can get the chessboard, princess," offered Natanael. The look on his face said he was praying she'd take the hint.

She didn't.

"Oh, forget chess, Nana," she tsked, using her favorite nickname for him. "I have a better game!"

Natanael groaned. "Princess, please, Colonel Mayleaf still hasn't grown all his eyebrows back yet from the last game we played. Don't you think it's a bit too soon for another one?"

"Oh silly, Nana," she said, patting him on the shoulder. "I have a much more interesting game than that."

"Just as long as it doesn't involve any fire, sharp metal objects, or," and at this, he shuddered. "Any more live fish from the pond," Natanael declared.

"No," Allonwë replied. "We are going to play a game I've made up called Hide and Scare!" Her face brightened the more she thought about it, the smile lighting up her eyes.

Natanael looked relieved for a moment, then frowned. "Who are we hiding from and scaring? Because if it's the king or queen again... I'm not getting fired over a game."

"Not 'we', Nana," giggled Allonwë. "Us! You seek; I'll hide and try to scare you before you find me. If I don't scare you before you find me and you tag me, you win. If you don't tag me but also don't get scared, I get another chance. But if you jump or get scared, I win, and it's your turn to scare me."

"I can't let you go wandering off by yourself, princess," disagreed Natanael.

True, she thought, there was no telling what kind of mischief she could get into on her own. Outwardly, however, she shrugged it off.

"Oh, Nana! You don't have to babysit me," she scoffed playfully.

"Will you stop calling me that?" he complained.

"Calling you what, Nana? Do you not like being called 'Nana', Nana? Oh, I'm, sorry, Nana, I should find something else to call my Nana, but it's so hard to change 'Nana' to something else when I'm so used to it, Nana!" she fired off, adding as many Nanas in her sentence as she could think to fit. She loved teasing him. "What about Tata?" she suggested brightly.

The look on Natanael's face was priceless. His demeanor suggested he was ready to settle down, sip on the oldest Elven wine, and contemplate his career path.

"I think," he managed at last. "I'll stick with Nana..."

"Splendid!" she chirped, clapping her hands together with glee. "Turn around and close your eyes."

"No!" he exclaimed, hands covering his backside.

The last time he did that, she'd put a fish down his pants and laughed til she cried as he danced around, trying to extract it and return it to the pond, getting sopping wet and muddy. And of course, it hadn't just been any old fish, it'd been one of the few that were big and had teeth. She'd apologized and felt horrible when he got scolded, and promised never to do it again. Apparently, it had left an impression.

"Just for five minutes while I go hide," she said, reassuring him by holding out her hands and showing him there were no fish to be found.

Natanael glared at her suspiciously.

"Please?" she added ever so sweetly, causing his resolve to waver.

"One minute," he replied at last with a sigh.

"Three," she bartered.

"Two and that's it," he consented, begrudgingly.

She could tell the look on her face was making him worry. Most people would see a bright, cheerful smile that would light up any room, but Natanael knew better. He saw an evil plot brewing behind her eyes and knew the second he agreed, he was going to get in over his head. As he turned around, she noticed he didn't remove his hands from his backside until she was at a safe distance. At that, she giggled. This would be a game he was good at, she mused. And perhaps it would help his bad mood out.

He'd been in a bad mood lately because of the preparations for the upcoming celebration between the Enarans and the elves of Kutawë. Taking care of her on top of everything else was overwhelming him, given how much effort went into ensuring the Enarans' safety. Hoping to lift his spirits during their playful antics, she also wanted to alleviate her own boredom.

Forcing herself to walk as calmly as possible so as not to attract attention, Allonwë made her way down the hall. There was an old tapestry in the west wing of the castle that would be perfect to hide and wait behind. Natanael was amazing at tracking her down whenever she played games like this.

It was only because Allonwë knew it flustered him so much that she would play these games. To be the guardian of the Elven princess of Kutawë and forced to play childish games with someone her age was most likely frustrating. He had to oblige her to keep her out of worse mischief whilst also making sure no one in the castle found out. Her parents were strictly no nonsense, and this added to Natanael's stress, for if caught, they'd both be scolded.

Allonwë, however, knew Natanael secretly welcomed the games they played because it broke up the monotony of everyday life at the castle. Without something to spice things up now and then, the atmosphere got both stale and oppressive. At least, to the younger elves, who were still full of energy and life. The older elves were more passive and never liked to do anything swiftly. A game of chess with an older elf could last months if they were feeling particularly passive. Allonwë couldn't stand sitting around like that for long periods of time. It drove her up the wall. This was why she had devised 'games' and 'adventures' for her and Natanael to go on when things got too boring around the castle.

There were fewer adventures compared to games because adventures often ended with something on fire.

Namely someone. And now, she was forced to sit in on fire safety classes every time they hired a new person in the kitchen.

After turning quite a few corners and making sure no one had seen her, Allonwë carefully slid behind the tapestry, making sure not to move it. Suppressing a cough as she stirred up some dust, she eased along the wall to get far enough away from the edge so any random passersby wouldn't see her. Natanael was probably searching for her already, and was most likely not that far behind.

Though she never picked the same hiding place twice, Natanael always found her rather quickly. It became more of a game to see how long she could hide from him before he found her, more so than *if* he'd find her. There was no 'if' in the matter. He always found her.

She smiled at the thought. Which meant if she ever really got lost and needed him, he'd always find her, she mused to herself, wiggling her bare toes happily. Something snagged the back of her dress on the wall. She felt behind her blindly to free herself, but couldn't quite reach it. She angled forward slightly, causing the tapestry to bulge so that she could reach her arm back far enough to get to the fabric without ripping it.

"Princess Allonwë?" came a voice from the hallway.

Allonwë straightened up suddenly and pressed herself against the wall as the voice continued.

"No, I haven't seen her. Is everything alright?"

The voice wasn't Natanael's, but she could tell he was there too from the inquiry.

Allonwë let out an involuntary yelp when the wall behind her suddenly gave way and she fell backwards into an empty space. She tumbled and rolled backwards down a slight slope until she came to a rather ungraceful, crashing stop on the dusty floor below. The sound of stone scraping on stone echoed in the room, revealing just how large the space actually was.

Allonwë sat up, coughing, and looked around, waving the dust she'd stirred up away from her face. It was a dark, windowless room, but her Elven eyes made it as clear as day until the torches lit themselves along the walls, making it eerie inside. There were shelves everywhere, and piles of trinkets and glittering things and scrolls and many valuable looking items, all covered in a rather thick layer of dust and cobwebs. Some things looked newer and had fewer cobwebs and less dust, but others looked so old she feared to touch them lest they turn to dust themselves.

She stood, brushing herself off as best she could, and stared at everything curiously. From the floor to the ceiling - also covered in dust and cobwebs - there were things to be seen glittering and twinkling, and aging and rusting. Allonwë stared in awe, having to remember to shut her gaping mouth. She shook her head and inspected the room. Two things in particular, though, caught her eye.

There was a painting in a niche on the wall, away from everything else, that caught her attention first. It depicted an elf in full body armor, holding his helmet in one hand and his sword in the other. On the sword was a bright, deep-sky blue jewel, embedded in the pommel. It reflected the fire in the elf's eyes.

The second thing that caught her attention was the pedestal of sorts beneath the painting. Atop the pedestal, something was hidden under a white silk cloth. Allonwë made her way over to the pedestal and hesitated. She was curious as to what this was, the existence of this entire room puzzled her.

Since when were there secret passages in this old castle? Sure, it was common enough in fairy tales and legends, but this wasn't the type of thing you found on just any old Thursday. Slowly, she reached out for the cloth - hesitating just a moment longer when a shiver of nervousness overtook her - then gently pulled it away.

Beneath the cloth was a red satin pillow, on top of which sat a silver bracelet with a gorgeous blue stone in it. The stone was the size of a large coin - almost large enough to be gaudy - and it fit so delicately in the bracelet which was woven with such an intricate pattern that Allonwë immediately fell in love with it. Almost entranced, she picked it up, and slid it onto her wrist and admired it. It was a perfect fit. There was a bright flash of fire from deep within the stone, and the silver, though cold against her skin, had a warmth all its own when you looked at it. There was no rust or tarnish. It gleamed beautifully. It was as if it had been laid there just moments before for someone to find.

For her to find.

When she put it on, something odd happened. The blue stone flashed and turned the same purple as her eyes, and Allonwë's heart sped up with excitement.

"Allonwë?" came the muffled sound of her name being called. "Princess Allonwë!"

Startled out of her reverie, Allonwë whirled around, heart sinking as she realized the opening she'd fallen through was closed off like it had never been there. She panicked as she called out and beat her fist against the wall. She didn't like being shut up in rooms with no windows or doors.

"In here! Get me out!" she yelled through the brick, praying someone could hear her. Being shut off with no way out suddenly made her lose her sense of curiosity about this room. All she was curious about now was finding an escape route.

"Princess?" came the startled, muffled reply from the other side of the wall. There was a moment of silence as she could imagine Natanael looking behind the tapestry in utter confusion.

"The wall opens somehow!" she yelled, the panic rising in her voice.

She didn't know what it was, but now that the opening was shut off, there was something about this room that was making her hair stand up on end. She wanted out of there now. The feeling was crawling up her spine, making her terrified of turning around lest she see whatever she feared to be true and alive in the room with her. If she wasn't alone in here, she didn't want to see what could survive in a room that looked like it hadn't been opened in decades.

Even elves could suffocate or starve to death.

"Where?" Natanael's voice commanded. He'd sensed her fear and was now on guard.

"I don't know-" she answered, taking very slight comfort in his tone. If anyone could protect her or get her out of dangerous situations, it was Natanael. As it was, her fear was growing out of hand. Her heart was pounding, skin was crawling, and the panic rising in the back of her throat was almost choking her. "Somewhere to the left of the-"

CRASH!

Allonwë's nerves were already on the brink of snapping, but the loud crash that came from behind her nearly sent her climbing the brick wall in front of her. She turned, pressed as far into the wall as she could make herself go, and searched for the source of the sound. From beneath a pile of glittering trinkets, a suit of golden armor carrying a sword stepped out of the debris and slowly seemed to get its bearings before turning its face toward her.

"Princess, are you al-" an ear-splitting scream from Allonwë cut Natanael's voice off.

That scream said all anyone needed to know. She wasn't playing games anymore. She could hear Natanael frantically beating on the wall in various places, trying to get the blasted thing to open, but failing. The soft thuds made her jump, thinking it was something else besides the armor coming after her, but then she realized they were Natanael's hands beating against the brick. She yelled at him to kick it down as the suit of armor came closer to her, its head wobbling dangerously right before it fell off to reveal nothing inside.

Another scream came from Allonwë as the haunted suit of armor came closer and closer, lifting its sword as if to fight her with it. Only she didn't have one. Something heavy seemed like it appeared in her hand and she looked down to see her hand wrapped around a sword handle that must have been laying against the wall. Picking it up, she held the sword out in front of her as if it would do anything to protect her on its own, and shook like a dog, terrified of being beaten.

Suddenly a thud behind her made the bricks give way and the door to the room opened again to reveal Allonwë and the now charging suit of haunted armor heading straight for her. Natanael darted in, grabbed her by the arm, hauling her out of there just before the wall swung shut again, blocking off the suit of armor and locking it in the room.

BAM!

The sound of the sword hitting the wall on the other side echoed in their ears. Allonwë was buried so far into Natanael's chest that she was pretty sure he couldn't see any of her face, and she was shaking so hard that she could barely stand.

Natnael set aside his own sword and comforted her,

checking if she was okay and if she'd been hurt. Thankfully, she hadn't and the sword she'd been holding was gone - probably dropped in the strange room when he'd grabbed her by the arm. When he'd calmed her down enough to talk, she explained how she'd gotten back there in the first place and the strange contents of the room.

"It all started when you called my name," she added shakily, sniffling back another fit of tears. "And I realized I was shut in with no way out." She wiped her face, embarrassed by the onslaught of tears that had overtaken her.

"Where did you get that?" Natanael asked, gently taking her wrist and looking at the bracelet as it was something new. He was always observant like that.

Allonwë stared at it a moment, uncomprehending at first. Then her mind pieced together the memory.

"I found it... in that room... I put it on and I was looking at it when you called me," she answered at last.

"I think you should take that off. It may be the reason whatever that was woke up and came after you," said Natanael.

Allonwë slung her arm away from her as if she thought the bracelet was cursed, then frantically began trying to pull the bracelet off. Whether the bracelet caused that thing to come after her didn't matter. If there was even the slightest chance that's what did it, she wanted nothing to do with it.

"It's stuck!" she yelled, her voice rising in pitch.

"Calm down! Calm down," Natanael quieted her. "Let me see it."

She pulled away from him just enough to hold out her wrist for him to see, as he turned it over several times, looking for a latch. Finding none, his brow furrowed as he gently tried to ease it off her wrist, but also without success. It was almost as if it were getting tighter each time they tried to pull it off.

Natanael sighed. "For now, let's just leave it alone. Hide it under your sleeve so your mother doesn't see it, and we will work on getting it off in a little while after you've calmed down. Meanwhile, we need to alert the castle to this room. There could be something more dangerous in there than a haunted suit of armor."

After Allonwë composed herself, she and Natanael informed the castle of the room and what happened, being sure to leave out certain details, like their game and the bracelet on Allonwë's wrist. Soon there were three mages, four guards, and several staff (most giving the area a wide berth) all gathered around the wall behind the torn down tapestry and murmuring amongst themselves. A hidden chamber in Sitani castle? Who'd ever heard of such a thing?

Allonwë and Natanael, however, were nowhere in sight of it. Outside the castle, wandering in the woods near the main crossroads, the princess and her bodyguard were arguing vehemently over how - or if - they should get the bracelet off Allonwë's wrist.

"You were the one who told me I should get it off in case that thing comes after me again!" Allonwë yelled as she tried to claw at the bracelet. She even took to biting it, which had Natanael smacking her hand away from her face to make her stop.

"Not if it means clawing and biting your wrist off with it!" Natanael yelled back, trying to keep her from making her already reddened skin turn bloody.

"Well, it won't come off!" she replied indignantly.

"See? This is what I mean when I tell you not to try on strange objects, princess. If you would just listen to me, we wouldn't have these problems!" he fussed at her, working on the bracelet himself.

"You make it sound like this is a habit for me," Allonwë accused darkly.

Natanael rolled his eyes. "Shall I remind you of the time you got your head stuck in the ceremonial flower vase at your grandfather's funeral because you said it looked like a-"

Allonwë cut him off. "I thought we agreed never to speak of that again!" she hissed, glancing around.

The thing about the vase at her grandfather's funeral wasn't what it sounded like. He'd died in a war when she was eight years old, and she had been in line with the family to go up to the casket and lay a flower on top of the lid before they buried him. It was then she'd noticed - not the ceremonial flower vase on the table near the casket (which incidentally looked like a wide mouthed fish) - but something on the far side of the table from one of her games she had been playing the previous day.

Not wanting her parents to know she had snuck into the chapel to play, she ducked under the tablecloth to come out the other side, grab it, stash it, and pretend as if nothing happened. Unfortunately, it didn't go as smoothly as she'd planned. The table cloth caught on some decorations in her hair, yanking the vase down when she tripped over her own feet, having been unable to see because of the cloth over her eyes. This caused the vase to topple over and land open end (or open-mouthed) over Allonwë's head.

Which wouldn't have been such a big deal if the tablecloth and flowers hadn't caused the vase to be a snug fit over her nose and mouth, or had the vase not been half filled with water for the flowers. Needless to say, there was a bit of a panic.

Natanael suppressed a mean grin, as if he were getting some kind of mirth from seeing her flustered for a change.

"Or the time you used the cloth thrown over his old chair as a cape, and it turned out someone put it there with a special powder on it to kill the insects in the cushion? You broke out in little red spots all over your-"

"Hold your tongue or I'll tell everyone that the reason the boar at last year's harvest festival tasted weird was because you-HMM-" Allonwë's mouth was covered by Natanael, who had let go of the bracelet and wrist and put both hands over her mouth.

"That's not fair. You put elderberry wine in my drink. You know how strong that stuff is and how susceptible I am to it," he hissed back, obviously embarrassed.

So much for getting her back. She pulled his hands away from her mouth and gave him a look.

"Then don't give me a reason to do it again," she retorted.

"You wouldn't," he said darkly. She lifted one eyebrow at him, keeping the other lowered in half a scowl. It said 'Try me. I dare you.' He knew better than to challenge her on this. It was usually just best to change the subject and distract her, lest she live up to that unspoken threat.

"Why did you try this bracelet on in the first place?" he sighed, turning away from her. She could tell he was getting frustrated. So much for alleviating his mood. He circled away from her, looking around at the trees as if they'd offer some kind of answer on how to get the bracelet off.

"I don't know!" she said defensively. "It didn't seem like such a bad idea at the time!"

"And now?" he muttered, obviously hoping she wouldn't hear. But oh, did she. Her elf ears never missed out on things he tried to mumble past her, and it was like he never learned that.

"Oh, forgive me for not having perfect foresight for everything!" she half snarled back, as she tried once again to pull the bracelet off her wrist using her teeth. The snarl wasn't so much towards Natanael as it was towards the blasted thing that was determined to stay on her wrist. But he wasn't entirely exempt, either. It had been so easy to slip on. Why was it being so difficult now?

"No worries - you have perfect hindsight," Natanael retorted, pulling her wrist away from her mouth again.

"ARGH!" she threw her hands up in defeat whilst silently wishing she could throw the thing as far away from her as possible. "Why won't this thing come OFF?" This stupid bracelet was becoming more trouble than it was worth.

"I hope we are not interrupting anything," came a voice from the direction of the road.

Both Allonwë and Natanael whirled around to see a small group of travelers - three in all - standing there watching their little frustrated argument. Allonwë straightened, and Natanael went on alert, stepping up beside her; both of them doing their best to fight off the determined blushes that threatened to spread across their faces. They had been hoping to come out here to keep from being overheard, but apparently there were still a few travelers out.

"A lover's quarrel, perhaps?" smiled the traveler who had spoken before.

Allonwë bristled at that.

"What are your reasons for coming here, travelers?" she demanded. "For you are deep within Elven country, and are not permitted to be here without good reason."

"Perhaps our being here, reasons being what they may, could help you out where you least expect it," countered the traveler.

Allonwë's face was now the mask of formality, her emotions under control.

Whatever these travelers wanted didn't matter. She would dismiss them from the property or have them forcibly escorted away. If they had slipped past the border guard and come all this way with no escort, they were up to no good. It also indicated that there was a need to improve security at the border.

"Be gone from this place immediately or you will be forcibly escorted-" she began.

"Now, now miss," interrupted the lead traveler, holding his hands up in a calming motion. "There's no need for all that. Just hear us out and we'll be on our merry little way, no trouble."

And if she didn't? Allonwë thought, eyeing them for a

moment, debating. She noticed Natanael's guard immediately go up. He didn't seem to trust this group or how they looked. Something in her gut said they should call for the guards right about now, but something made her stop. If they called backup, the castle would find out about the bracelet. Her eyes flickered to it and she brought her sleeve down over it. One traveler followed her gaze and flickered back up to hers, just as she looked back at them.

Natanael's hand went to his sword, and he stared them down. No one just waltzed into Kutawë. Especially not acting as if it were a normal occurrence. She noted the one to the left of their leader met Natanael's warning with a steady gaze.

The look said they weren't afraid of a fight, and that made Allonwë's hair stand up on the back of her neck. Only a person who was self-assured in their fighting capabilities and had the competence to support that self-assurance refrained from bragging when encountering someone else getting ready for a fight.

She noted their clothing, all loose, gray rag-like robes, hiding any sort of physique - preventing anyone from judging how well built they were. The look in the left traveler's eye made her nervous. It said 'Don't do it.' It didn't boast about them not standing a chance. Didn't size Natanael up, deciding if he could take the elf on in a fight. That look knew Natanael didn't stand a chance, and that made Allonwë's gut scream internally for them to call back up.

But they couldn't. Not if they wanted to keep the bracelet a secret.

"I think it's best if we leave now, m'lady," Natanael muttered, barely above a whisper to Allonwë. She knew he didn't dare call her princess in front of these men, in case they would take advantage of that. Calling her princess in front of such people would tell them everything they needed to know if they were brigands.

Debating for a moment, Allonwë considered her options.

She mostly agreed with Natanael, but anything to avoid conflict with these people to leave peacefully would be better than making a huge scene. Especially if such a huge scene brought attention as to why she was out here in the first place, and why she had a mysterious bracelet on her wrist. She eyed them for a moment, then took a breath.

"I will hear them out," she announced, to Natanael's dismay.

The lead traveler bowed graciously with a smile.

"My lady," he purred, making Allonwë frown in disgust. "To be quite frank, we are looking for food, or some money with which to buy some. Would the lady have anything to spare for poor travelers?"

"I'm sorry, but I have no money or food on me," replied Allonwë. "Perhaps you could find some in the next-"

"Perhaps we could barter," the lead traveler said quickly, cutting her off. "The lady has such a lovely bracelet. It could fetch enough for all three of us to eat several meals. Surely a lady as grand as yourself would have many like it or better and could spare it?"

"This?" Allonwë asked suspiciously. "Why this, of all things?"

"We couldn't very well ask the lord here for his nice shiny dagger, in fear he'd run us through with it," replied the lead traveler with a chuckle.

"Awfully scary, that one," added the third traveler from behind his hand in an almost comical gesture, as if to hide it from Natanael, though he could see and hear it as plainly as Allonwë could.

"And what do you have to barter for this bracelet that I should agree to such a thing?" she asked.

"Perhaps a game of chance?" the lead traveler suggested. "Should you win, we will give you a trade in knowledge. Of something coming your way. Should you lose, we get the bracelet and go about our merry way," replied the lead traveler.

Allonwë's eyes lit up. She always liked the sound of a game.

"I don't like it," growled Natanael by her ear. Then, to the travelers, said, "What's coming our way?"

"That would be for you to find out in our game of chance," the lead traveler said.

"They could be swindlers. I suggest we leave and not give them any-" Natanael began.

"Oh Nana, it's not like it'll come off anyhow," Allonwë murmured back. "And besides, if they do win and can get it off, then hey, they get to eat. It's not like this old thing has caused anything but trouble." Then, before Natanael could stop her, she stepped forward to meet the travelers. "What kind of game?"

The travelers smiled.

Lesson 2

∽

SHINY OBJECTS AREN'T ALWAYS YOUR FRIEND

"Whoa!" exclaimed Allonwë. "It just came off!"

The annoying bracelet that had forcibly latched onto her wrist like a hungry predator had finally relinquished its death grip on her. But why? How? It was almost as if losing the bet had made it come loose. The instant she lost it had relinquished its grip on Allonwë like something giving up a fight.

"How'd you do that?" Natanael asked suspiciously.

"I pulled," replied the lead traveler with a chuckle. There was no way it could have been that easy. Something had to be up.

Allonwë shot him a look that screamed for a fight, but Natanael spoke back up.

"You've won it fair and square. Now be on your way," he said.

"No need to be so hasty, young master," said the leader, his drawl of the Western regions coming through heavily. "We've no wish to cause you ill." He gave a wink and a chuckle as he turned, lifting the bracelet up to indicate it. "Good day to you both! And thank you for your patronage!"

Allonwë looked on as Natanael watched them go. She

could tell he had a sinking feeling in his gut the further away they got from the worry lines that formed on his face. He was probably certain he was going to regret this later if her parents found out he'd let their daughter bet with a trio of common travelers and lost a bracelet of unknown origin and value.

Probably prayed the border guard wouldn't stop and question them about it. If they mentioned anything about him or Allonwë, it would come back to bite him in both the paycheck and the proverbial ass. Her parents didn't approve of her being or doing anything less than ladylike, and betting (with commoners, no less) certainly was far from that ideal image.

On the way back, Natanael made sure Allonwë knew just how badly he felt about the situation for the entire fifteen-minute walk back to the castle.

"You always do this Allonwë. You play a game or go on an adventure as you call them and I get dragged into it because I can't let you go unguarded, and we always end up in trouble." Natanael was saying. "You're smarter than this. I don't know why you pretend you're an airhead in front of everyone - even me sometimes - when it suits you better to actually use that clever mind of yours for the good of the many rather than just yourself!"

Allonwë finally, fed up with all his nagging, threw her hands up in frustration at him.

"Because I'm not ready to take on the responsibilities of the court, Nana! I'm terrified of what it means to take on the role of ruler in this country. What does it matter if I'm smart if I'm incapable of taking care of the lives of the thousands of people I'll be responsible for? That's a terrifying weight, don't you think? The whole kingdom! On *my* shoulders! Me? Absolutely not. Could *you* do it?"

"I'm just a guard," Natanael stammered, taken aback by her statement.

"And I'm just one person! So, yes! I'm going to continue to be air-brained to put off taking on those responsibilities for as long as I possibly can because there's no chance in the five hells that I'm ready for that kind of role." Allonwë turned on her heel and continued up the side of the hill they were climbing to Sitani castle.

Natanael hesitated, but followed, obviously not certain how to follow up with that. She had a point, and she'd driven it home. At least, she hoped she had. She was tired of hearing about it.

When they reached one of the main thoroughfares, the palace was in an uproar.

"What's going on?" Allonwë asked one of the servants wringing her hands as she watched the crowd gathered around the secret room Allonwë had discovered.

"Someone's stolen something," she said, addressing Allonwë in formal speech with a bow and a squeak. "Something of great importance."

"What exactly?" Allonwë asked, noting the servant's nervous glance back over her shoulder and subsequent hesitation.

"I'm not sure, but from what I can understand, there are a few things. A bracelet, a stone, and a weapon of great power."

Allonwë mentally prayed the bracelet she had found wasn't the one they were in such a tizzy about, but with her luck it would be the exact one for which they were looking. How important could one stupid bracelet be? Seemed she'd find out soon enough.

"Oh what are we going to do?" the servant asked, worried. "What if they use the weapon on us?"

Before Allonwë could comment, another servant came and announced her parents were summoning her to question her about the room that she had discovered. She exchanged glances with Natanael, noting the wary look on his face that said 'I told you so'. Beaming her best cheerful, carefree smile at him to counteract it, even winking at him where the servants couldn't see. She turned, following said servant to the chamber where her parents were waiting for her. Couldn't have Natanael be too worried, could she? She was getting worried enough for the both of them.

Her parents stood at a table pouring over some scrolls, muttering to each other. Her father, in his usual colorful ceremonial robes, was a giant; towering bald head and shoulders over his wife and daughter (and at least half a head over the tallest of their guards). He kept his head shaven because he served as one of the spiritual leaders for their country; the crown passing down through the female line. Her mother, in more reserved colors that went well with her hair and eyes, stood beside her husband, tucked into one of his long, brawny arms.

She pursed her lips in thought, her brow furrowing. Of her two parents, Allonwe took mostly after her mother in appearance, even though her mother's hair was a dark earthy brown. Her eyes were the same color as Allonwë's - that deep purple that ran in their bloodline. It was said to appear in those who would become prominent leaders of their time, but they dismissed this as folly by the time Allonwë turned seven.

When she entered, the servant announced her presence, and her parents looked up.

"Ah! Allonwë, dear, just who we needed to see," her father said, beckoning her over.

As she moved forward, the servant took his leave, closing the door behind Allonwë and sealing her in alone with her parents, cutting off her only escape. This was just as bad as the secret room, Allonwë thought. Then mentally prayed the bracelet she lost wasn't important.

"Dear," her mother began. "When you stumbled across that room, did you see a bracelet with a red jewel in it?"

Allonwë brightened instantly as she remembered the bracelet she'd found and then bartered away had been decorated with a blue, then a purple jewel, not a red one.

She mentally noted to do a dance when her parents

weren't watching because for once, she wasn't getting in trouble for something she did!

Out loud, however, she stated, "No, mother. I did not."

"Did you notice one in there anywhere at all? This is important, dearest," her mother urged.

"It would have been shiny," her father added. "I know you're keen on shiny things."

Allonwë bit back the retort that his head was shiny, but she wasn't too keen on that. Instead, she held her tongue and kept her face as blank as she could. Instead of retorting, she pretended to think on it very hard, before replying that no, she had seen nothing of the sort, then asked couldn't they just buy another one like it if it meant so much?

Her parents had mixed looks on their faces at the question. Her father looked as if he were wondering if he should take the time and explain the difference between one kind of value and another, yet not really wanting to reveal what was so important about the bracelet. However, her mother wasn't buying the air brained act and was shooting her a look that told her to act her age. She also seemed to question her daughter's intelligence for asking such a ridiculous question. At least the crossed arms, eye rolling, and heavy sigh told Allonwë that much.

They asked her a few more questions before dismissing her, not having gleaned any useful information from her answers. She gladly took her leave and left the room, closing the door mostly shut behind her, and glancing around to see if anyone was watching. When she determined the coast was clear, she pressed herself against the closed door and peeked around the opening to see her parents talking quietly amongst themselves, but not so quietly she couldn't hear them.

She was determined to find out what was really going on. When her parents withheld information from her like her father had just done, it immediately piqued her curiosity. She knew he was hiding something, because her father was notorious for his inability to hide what he was thinking. His thoughts and emotions played across his face so openly anyone could read them.

This was why all of Allonwë's birthday presents were surprises for the both her and her father.

It was also another reason her mother was the one who dealt with public and foreign relations. There were just certain faces you couldn't make out loud like that.

Besides, this was the first interesting thing that had happened around here in years! Well, that Allonwë hadn't caused, at least. There was no chance she was going to miss it.

Inside the room, she caught the sound of her mother sighing. It was a distinct sound that always came after one of Allonwë's shenanigans. It was a sigh she'd grown to hate to hear directed at her because it meant she'd disappointed her mother and her mother was going to pull a guilt trip on her. Until she made things right again, at least. Hopefully she would not get punished for this, since she actually had done nothing wrong this time.

"It's alright, dearest," came her father's voice. "She was most likely so terrified when that suit of armor came after her she doesn't recall most of the details. I know I would have been-"

"It's not the suit of armor!" her mother's irritated voice cut him off. "It just feels like there's something she's leaving out on purpose. I just don't know what or why."

"What makes you say that?" asked her father.

"I know our daughter," her mother replied, as if it were obvious.

"What do you mean?" her father reiterated.

"She's not the air-brained twit she would have the courts believe she is," her mother scolded. "She has moments of questionable judgment, but-"

"Like the time she wanted to learn how to breathe fire by spitting wine into a torch?" supplied Allonwë's father.

Allonwë winced.

"Yes!" nodded her mother. "That poor elf is still trying to grow all of his hair back."

"Ah, yes, Colonel Mayleaf," the king agreed.

"You know she used the dress we wanted her to wear at the harvest festival as material to light the torch?" informed the queen. "The one she hated?"

"That's what happened to it?" the king gasped in surprise. "Wait, she told me she liked that dress..."

"She was trying to spare your feelings, dear," comforted the queen. "Though I daresay she could have done that without setting fire to the thing. She devised a way to direct the attention away from what she was really doing, by creating a story that supported her air-brained persona."

"Really?" the king asked, surprised. "Clever girl..." he muttered, rubbing his bearded chin. "Do you suppose she really knows something about the missing artifact?"

"I don't know," Allonwë's mother sighed. "The Dragon-fell Stone is a very dangerous weapon. I'm not even sure she knows what it does. And if she doesn't know what it does, then to her it would just be a shiny trinket. Even though she likes those things, she's smart enough to know that if she takes something like that, there's nothing she can do with it without getting caught. She couldn't wear it without being seen, and she couldn't hide it in the castle without the servants finding it when they cleaned."

Reason number one why Allonwë didn't keep a diary.

"Do you think she really knows nothing about it?" Allonwë's father asked.

"Oh, I didn't say that," her mother replied. "Just because she is smart enough to know she'd get caught if she ever stole it, doesn't mean she doesn't know where it's gotten off to. She's probably still trying to devise a way to divert the brunt of the blame away from herself. Whatever she's not telling us, I'm sure it will lead us to where the weapon is."

"Good luck to us getting it out of her then," the king muttered, half to himself, half to his wife. "I just hope we can before it's too late and something happens."

"Give it time," the queen replied. "I'm sure we'll get something out of her. I just hope it's before the celebration tomorrow. We can't let the Enarans know we've lost the weapon, it'll cause mass panic."

Allonwë heard footsteps moving towards the door and skittered away before she could get caught. So, her mother knew about the dress she'd burned? Hideous thing it was. She didn't regret burning it. And she would have gotten away with it had someone not walked around the corner at the most inopportune of moments. It made her wonder just what else her mother knew about her schemes.

With her thoughts swirling, she made her way to the library. There had to be something in there about the Dragonfell Stone thing they mentioned.

Upon entering the library, she quickly sought out the magic and history sections, carefully choosing books that she believed would provide her with the desired information. As she flipped through them, she set each one aside when she realized it wasn't important. For a solid half hour, she diligently scoured through a multitude of sources, immersing herself in a sea of information until she stumbled upon a somewhat useful excerpt in a book chronicling the evolution of weaponry.

"In the Great Elf and Dragon Wars, Lord Noland used a weapon of great power that was said to have been created from a Heart Stone.[1] Used to defeat the very creatures it was created from, Lord Noland led the elves in an attack against the Great Dragons who ravaged the land without mercy."

Allonwë flipped the page only to find this was all that was written about the mysterious weapon. She checked the footnote that was listed in the description.

"[1] A Heart Stone is a stone that forms from the last drop of blood that falls from a dragon's fatal wound. Hardening into a

ruby-like jewel that can be anywhere from the size of a pea to the size of a grown man's fist, the Heart Stone contains an enormous amount of power that is neither good nor evil, and depends on its current wielder to determine if its color will change."

Allonwë's brow furrowed. It can change colors? A theory formed in her mind, one that she was afraid to prove true. She looked up from her seat on the floor and checked a few volume names before dumping her lapful of books and running off to a section of magic and healing, only stopping to grab a few books on dragons in the science section on the way. Once her arms were loaded, she made her way back to her section in the history department, shooing away a librarian who was attempting to put some books she'd gathered back on the shelf. Apologizing profusely, he bowed and ducked away, but Allonwë ignored him, plopping down on the floor again and scouring the books for a reference on Heart Stones.

How could it change colors and why? What powers did it possess? Or did that depend on the wielder and it was just an infinite power source? Or was it infinite at all? Could it be used continually? Or would its power run out? If it ran out, could it be recharged?

She let her mind wander a bit as she flipped through a few of the books and tossed them aside when they proved to be useless. Finally, she located an excerpt on them in a book of magic, under a section titled 'Instruments and Spell Enhancers' that read:

"A Heart Stone: both a thing of magic and a tool of magic. Can power a spell(s), expedite the healing process, or be used to channel one's own power and amplify it, etc. A Heart Stone can be used as a tool, but is also somewhat like a living thing. When wielded, it is said to have a live, animal-like feel to it, resting, breathing, heart beating against one's skin.

Although it is said the lifespan of a Heart Stone is as long as the life of the dragon[3] it came from, this theory has remained untested. For as of the writing of this, there has not been a Heart

Stone around long enough to discover the truth of this. Some stones have existed, but have had their life force either extinguished in one great spell, or stolen back by the dragon kind.

Heart Stones are one of the few formidable offenses and defenses against a dragon attack. Dragon defenses are weaker toward a power like their own than against an opposing one. Lord Noland[4] wielded one recorded weapon, which used a Heart Stone as its source of power in the first and second Great Dragon Wars. This weapon, also known as The Armor of the King[5], the Sword of Noland[6], or The Dragonfell Stone[7], was combined with the Spell of Asai[8] to create a special defense and great offense in battle. When formed[9], the Heart Stone takes on the color of a deep blood red, but can change to a color that reflects the use to which it is put.[10]"

Allonwë's eyes skipped to footnote number ten, which stated:

"[10]If applied to a defensive spell, it may take on a peaceful color during a peaceful moment, whereas if an attack came, it would flash a dark warning color. Lord Noland's weapon did this. The stone on the hilt of his sword would be blue in times of peace, but blood red as a newly formed Heart Stone when danger was near or present. It was also said that when not in full armor, the sword would take on a different shape that would be easily worn, so that Lord Noland could keep it on his person."

It could change shape! And the color depended on the spell and how it reacted to peace or war. She briefly wondered if there was such a spell that would make it turn rainbow colored, but shook her head and focused her thoughts.

So, if it could change into a bracelet, and it only changed colors when danger was near, that meant the bracelet she had found might be the one they were looking for so desperately. But why? That probably explained why it changed its color to red when she gave it to the travelers...

So, he had a shapeshifting weapon that could turn from a

sword to a bracelet. Not very impressive. Besides, couldn't they create more of those easily? Or could they? Was the spell that hard to create? What was the spell of Asai exactly, and what did it do? Glancing at footnote number eight, she noted it listed what page number she could look up the spell of Asai.

Flipping to it, she found a detailed description of how to set it up, the tools and ingredients needed for the spell, how much power it took, the level of difficulty (medium) and, what she was looking for, an explanation of what it did.

The Spell of Asai: creed by the Mages of Barlow[15] in the 22nd year of the Age of Balbadûr to arm their best soldiers against the Archmage and Necromancer, Sheldane of Jesherir.[16]

Spell type: Defensive, Arming, Personal.

Function: This spell can create a partial or full body armor around the wielder when danger is near. When the wielder needs to fight back, this spell provides a personal weapon of the wielder's choice (such as a sword or spear) in order to defend themselves or others around them. This spell cannot cover more than one person at a time, unless fueled by a powerful alternative source.[17]

Warning! Do not use it in defense against dragons! This weapon is not a dragon fire[18] resistant, or dragon spell[19] resistant. By itself, this spell can only defend against humanoid attacks, such as elves, dwarves, humans, goblins, trolls, and other such creatures and creature-made weapons. Anything greater will need a significant amount of power in order to defend against.

So, the Heart Stone was what made the spell able to defend against dragons! Okay, that was a bit more impressive. Especially since every story she ever heard that contained a dragon, they were these enormous, horrifying, and brutal beasts of legend. There was a reason there had been three all-out wars between elves and dragons. The dragons kept terrorizing the elves' villages, and the elves sought vengeance for stolen livestock, dead villagers, and losing several towns.

"There you are!"

Allonwë shrieked and dropped the book she had her nose buried in. Natanael had snuck up on her without her noticing. Surrounded by the piles of books she'd been digging through, Allonwë looked like she was building a miniature fort out of colorfully bound volumes. Natanael probably wouldn't put that past her, come to think of it, she realized.

"What are you doing?" he asked.

Allonwë stood up abruptly, looked around, smiled nervously at a lone bewildered librarian staring at her, and waved at him.

"Uh, could you please put these back? I have an urgent matter I need to attend to. Thanks!" Allonwë declared.

And with that, she leaped over the piles of books she'd gathered, grabbed Natanael's wrist and hauled him out of the library

"A-Allonwë! It's rude to just leave a pile of books for the librarian to clean up!" Natanael stammered, trying to keep up, but it was a futile effort on his part to get her to slow down.

Ignoring him yet again, she left the library and led him down the servants' halls until they came outside into a small courtyard garden empty of anyone but them. Once she could breathe again, having run the whole way, she began frantically to tell Natanael of what she'd learned.

"What if it really was the bracelet they are looking for?" she asked once all the words had tumbled out of her mouth. "What are we going to do and how can we get it back? Mother knows I'm hiding something, and she somehow found out about the dress that I set fire to, so she knows I'm capable of scheming! And I don't want this to come out where everyone hears about it! They'll think if I'm old enough to come up with stuff this elaborate, then I'm old enough to start taking on responsibilities of the court and expect me to do boring stuff all the time! Like public and foreign relations. Not to mention getting married to some high-ranking old elf who's going to expect me to pop out children! Now I'm going to get in trouble for the bracelet that's missing and who knows what other hell is going to rain down on my head. I don't want to marry an old guy and have his children. If he's really old, he'll have really long ears and really long ears are really gross!" Allonwë was speaking so fast and high pitched that Natanael couldn't quite understand all that she was saying judging from the look on his face. He could read her panic, but then, she could read his too.

"This is exactly what I was talking about! No more games ever!" he hissed through clenched teeth, followed by a chorus of 'evers' driving his point home. "This is what you get me into every time! So help me, if you weren't the princess-" He jabbed his finger at her, the rest of his sentence so garbled from irritation that the words were no longer distinguishable.

"Look, it's not my fault!" argued Allonwë. "I had no idea Colonel Mayleaf was going to be coming around the corner right when I spit the wine into the torch! And besides, his hair has started to grow back!" she added, thinking about what her parents had mentioned about the man that was still recovering.

If anything, she was also a victim because people wouldn't stop bringing it up. Can't a person just live down a mistake without having it thrown back in their face over and over? It had been an accident!

"Sure, he's still missing a few patches, and perhaps his eyebrows will never fully recover, but at least he still has his face! I nearly lost mine!" Allonwë complained.

She had come dangerously close to setting herself on fire when the surprise of suddenly seeing someone standing there that hadn't been there before, and most definitely wasn't supposed to be, hit her, and the wine spilled out of her mouth when she tried to shout a warning.

"I think it's unfair to keep hounding me about that! People are completely overreacting."

"I was referring," Natanael replied, giving her an incredulous look. "To the fact that you bartered a priceless family heirloom and highly dangerous weapon of enormous power off to a random group of travelers we've never met before, and will probably never see again because they've skipped town, country! Meanwhile, the person they sold the thing to is off conquering the rest of the free world!" Natanael took a breath. "But now that you mention it, thanks to that little stunt you pulled with the torches and the wine, I also have Colonel Mayleaf breathing proverbial fire down my back to figure out what the hell happened. But you're still dancing around the castle devising new and improved ways of torturing me! So no, I don't think I'm overreacting!"

"Keep your voice down. Someone will hear us," she reminded him. "And let's figure something out!" she added, feeling snappish. "Rather than standing here and blaming people for stuff, why don't we figure out how to get it back?"

"And how do you propose we do that?" Natanael argued, with a tone that said he knew full well she was the only one to blame.

"You're a skilled tracker. We'll go after it," Allonwë suggested.

"Absolutely not!" Natanael balked, as if she were suggesting something stupid. "You are not going on a dangerous mission like this, and don't even suggest me going alone," he cut her off as soon as she opened her mouth. "My duty is to protect you and keep you out of harm's way! And I know if I went, you'd try to follow me anyhow."

"Fine then," Allonwë quipped. "I'll go and you'll have to follow me."

"I said no!" Natanael said firmly. "Not only is it too dangerous, but we'd never get out of the castle without getting stopped by a thousand guards who would all want to know why you and I are sneaking off. Neither of us wants to explain to them what we're doing, nor who's responsible for losing it."

"We can't let them get away, and we can't tell everyone who has it. No one knows where to look except us, so we are the only ones that can get it back," Allonwë argued.

"We can't!" Natanael repeated, exasperated. "We'd never get out of the castle. I'd be slaughtered for even considering letting you go, and your parents would disown you if they knew not only what you've done, but what you are planning to do."

"If you can make that last one a promise, then we are most definitely doing this," Allonwë quipped. "Besides, we'll just wait until tomorrow when everyone is busy at the summer festival, and the guards are doing their duty to my parents. I'll say I have a headache, go lay down, change clothes, meet you in the eastern servant courtyard where no one will see us because everyone will be greeting the envoy from Enara, and we'll head out in the middle of the night when they least expect it! They will preoccupy themselves with the festival and trying to allude that everything is normal, that they won't even think about the two of us until we are a good day and a half journey ahead! If not more... And, if we start out early enough, we can catch up to the travelers!"

Natanael opened and closed his mouth several times, trying to come up with an argument she'd listen to. Suddenly, recognizing the plan's viability.

"I'm going no matter what," continued Allonwë. "And you can either stay here and let me go by myself and face the wrath of my parents now, or you can go with me to protect me from harm, help me track down the travelers, and when we return with the bracelet, and be revered as heroes."

Natanael sighed and rubbed his face, looking as if he'd aged a decade in that moment. On the one hand, they both knew if he tried to stop her, the travelers got away with the bracelet. Who knew what could happen? She'd find some way to slip away and go after them, knowing full well he'd try to save her in the process. She'd probably get lost, and nearly get herself killed out there on her own, and he'd get in serious trouble when he dragged her back to the castle for letting her get away.

If he followed her plan, faced the odds of finding the bracelet again, and returned before the royal search party killed him for not bringing her back immediately... her shenanigans would likely get them killed in the process.

So it was a stay here, be killed. Go with her and possibly be killed, but also come back with the bracelet and potentially not be killed.

Allonwë watched all this unfold on his face and smiled when he sighed, beaming happily at him.

"I'll meet you two hours after sunset tomorrow!" she chirped happily, clapping her hands and skipping away. "Don't be late!" she called in a sing-song voice as he watched her go.

"I didn't agree to this!" he hissed after her.

"Don't be late!" she repeated, disappearing around the corner and leaving him probably wondering what he'd gotten himself into once again.

Lesson 3

SAILORS MAKE GREAT PARTY GUESTS

The one thing about these celebrations Allonwë could always count on was the fact they would last until dawn, then the preparations for the after feast held the next day at high noon would begin. They spent the first day in boisterous partying that led to drunken elves singing ballads and (if they were drunk enough) dancing with various potted plants if they couldn't find a suitable partner; followed by a day of a peaceful meal time to reflect on the specific focus of whichever particular celebration was coming next.

Generally, Allonwë enjoyed these celebrations because they were the only thing that ever caused people to forget the rules of proper behavior, throw caution to the wind, and act silly for once in their dull lives. They didn't come nearly often enough, in her opinion, nor get as silly as she would prefer to see, but she made the most of what she could get seeing as the other most interesting thing to do was either a good game of chess or nature walk. And there's only so many times a stir-crazy elf can play chess before she's ready to incinerate the pieces in some ingenious plot that would banish the game from ever being played again.

(This is also why Allonwë was so well acquainted with the forests surrounding Sitani castle.)

This time, however, she was in for a real adventure. She settled into her seat, overlooking the opening ceremonies of the first parade of the night. They had a sister clan coming to visit tonight. It was the elves from Enara from the eastern seashores. Sailors! Damn - tonight would have been a good one to attend. Too bad she was going to have to miss it. Ah well, at least she might get a chance to use her sword fighting on this trip. Natanael had been teaching her sword fighting and a bit of archery since he first became her bodyguard. It hadn't done her much good recently. The only thing she could focus on in that hidden room was her blind fear and over-whelming desire to get out of there unscathed from that suit of armor.

Hopefully, that wouldn't hinder her in the next fight. She'd have to learn how to move past the fear. Meanwhile, she needed to figure out how to get away. However, even after a good solid half hour of begging her mother to let her leave, getting out if the ceremony was proving harder than Allonwë expected. Her mother seemed determined to keep her here, even if it killed her. Which, if you could die from impatience and anticipation, Allonwë was sure her life was drawing to a close.

She mentally bemoaned her situation as if they were her last dying thoughts.

What was so important about this festival over all the other festivals that required her presence? They usually got along just fine, with or without her. Why was the one time she wanted to get away-

Wait... Did her mother know what she was planning? Had Natanael squealed? ...No, that didn't sound like something he'd do. Had someone overheard them? Curse those overzealous servants! They probably followed to make sure all was okay, overheard everything, and felt obligated to tell the king and queen!

(Like that one instance when she told her Enaran friend, Elias, how she numbered three chickens one, two, and four and set them loose in the castle and had the whole castle in an uproar looking for the chicken labeled 'three' but it didn't exist. Elias had laughed so hard he cried, watching the servants get so mad at her when they found out. The servants promptly told her parents once they overheard her diabolical scheme, and she was scolded yet again.)

She sat up straight, a string of unladylike dwarven curses that she'd picked up in a book running through her mind. If that were the case, then she would have to figure out how to escape when no one was looking. Trick was learning how to avoid her mother's 'third eye' detection.

Allonwë swore that her mother had eyes in the back of her head sometimes. How else could she see the things Allonwë did when her back was turned? She'd once tried to look for them while pretending to play with her mother's hair. She'd had no luck finding them, of course, but that hadn't stopped her from looking several times as a child. What if her mother's second set of eyes had somehow learned of tonight's plans and she was purposely keeping her here in order to thwart them?

"Mother, please," she tried once more, softly, trying to sound as ill as she could. "I just want to go lie down."

"You can lie down when this ceremony is over," quipped her mother, getting irritated with her persistence. "Now, be silent! It's about to begin!" she added in a whisper.

"That's why I want to leave now, so I don't seem rude!" Allonwë tried to argue, but it was too late. Down below, the music heralded the start of everything. She and her parents were sitting on a raised platform overlooking the festival. There were hundreds of elves in colorful clothing, lanterns of all shapes and sizes hanging everywhere, music blaring with performers wearing bells and ribbons on their wrists and ankles dancing about. The sound of laughter, clapping, cheers, and drumming echoed off the buildings and hills. An entourage marched into formation before the platform, the crowd parting to give them room. The music and noise from the crowd ceased, and the queen stood, followed by her husband and daughter.

"Greetings, brethren, from the eastern shores! We welcome you with open arms and thank you for coming," the queen began. This was nothing out of the ordinary. The same thing happened every time one of the sister Elven clans came to a festival. They gave the same speech and had the same celebration. The primary purpose of their arrival was mostly for relationships.

Elvish clans that aided Noland in the Great Elf and Dragon Wars would come every so often and renew their friendship with the elves of Kutawë. The elves of Enara had been the closest friends and allies, coming almost once a year since the end of the wars. It probably also had something to do with the bad weather this time of the year brought to the eastern shore area. It was Allonwë's theory that they just came mostly to escape the horrid storms that raged across the beaches.

Still, she didn't mind seeing Elias again. Elias was the prince of Enara. They had grown up together, and he always helped her get in and out of shenanigans. Maybe she could rope him into helping her tonight! He was great with coming up with stories on the fly and making them sound believable.

He might be able to help her get away from her mother long enough to escape into the night. Hopefully, her mother knowing about what happened to the bracelet wouldn't make it completely impossible to get out of there and get it back. Hopefully, it also wouldn't get Natanael fired, she thought with a wince. Even if Elias could buy them just a few hours before the Sitani castle realized they were missing, it would be a tremendous help.

As Allonwë plotted how to make everything work out, her mother had continued in her ceremonial greeting speech, reaching the part where both sides moved forward to greet each other in the midway platform. The Enara family walking up, while the Kutawë family walked down.

Elias was a good six feet tall give or take, as dark-skinned as earth, and had short cropped sun-bleached blonde hair that never liked to lie down properly because of the amount of salt water it absorbed. He was muscular, as were most of the sea elves that worked on boats, and it showed under the simple over the shoulder ceremonial robes he was wearing. The sea was something that Elias loved dearly. He couldn't understand how Allonwë could stand to be amongst trees all the time.

"You can't see anything around you, and you can't see the stars," he'd said.

"You could," she'd replied once. "If you tried climbing one like those masts that you climb all the time."

But it wasn't the same.

"Out on the sea," he'd once told her. "If the waters are calm, and it's a clear night, it's like you are floating in a sea of stars."

It was one of his favorite feelings in the world.

Allonwë and Elias hugged like old friends do, and she whispered their key phrase that alerted the other to when a shenanigan could be, would be, or was currently afoot.

"Storm's a brewin'," she said.

"Fine night for a good wind," he replied with a wink, acknowledging he'd understood, and smiled.

He had a handsome smile. It was growing more and more mature. (Even though he was at least a few years older than Allonwë, she always thought he looked too young for his age.)

"And now!" declared Allonwë's mother, Lady Alannah, to the crowd. "For our special announcement!" Allonwë's brow furrowed. Special announcement? Was that what her mother had been keeping her here for? Had she not found out about tonight's shenanigans after all? Or did she, and this was just something that Allonwë was going to be roped into so that she really couldn't go anywhere for the rest of the night without getting in a ton of trouble and insulting their sister clan?

"For generations, the elves of Kutawë and the elves of Enara have been close friends and allies. Whenever Kutawë needed aid, Enara was there to lend a hand. I hope we have been generous friends in return and showed our support as eternally. We are grateful to our sister clan, and thank you for all you have done for us, and declare that tonight, we wish to strengthen that bond!" her mother continued.

How can they strengthen it any more than- Oh. Oh no. She turned and glared at Elias. Did he know about this? Elias looked as confused and alarmed as she did. In fact, he was giving her the same accusing look as if to ask, "Did you know about this?" but neither of them had. This was all their parent's doing. Allonwë paled. They wouldn't. They couldn't! "With the betrothal of our daughter, Allonwë Avonmora Nïahm, Princess of Kutawë to Lord Neo Teo Quinn's son, Elias Teo Quinn, Prince of Enara, our two countries shall be joined as one, forever united!"

The crowd cheered.

Allonwë looked at Elias and stumbled slightly as she literally rocked backward from the shock. They had just forcibly betrothed her to her childhood friend. She still had to get out of there. She still had to find Natanael and go after the bracelet. Natanael - where was he? She didn't want to be here right now. She wanted to be anywhere but there, and she wanted Natanael with her. He'd know what to do, he always knew what to do. She wanted to bolt and start their journey right away, not caring who knew now, but she couldn't think straight. How could she get away from all this noise and get her thoughts in order?

In the split second that passed and these thoughts ran through her mind, she looked at Elias, who had stepped toward her when he saw her stumble slightly. She had an idea. She did the only thing she could think of to buy them both some time.

She fainted.

Or at least pretended to, right into Elias's arms, who scrambled to catch her. Calling for help, he lifted her up with ease. Everyone scrambled to help her, panicking, and in no time, they had rushed her to her room and laid her in her bed. Servants, personal maids, her parents, a couple of doctors, and Elias all packed into her room, checking on her, asking if she was okay, and trying to make a general sense of what was going on.

～

Natanael, having witnessed the whole thing, caught up with them and shooed everyone but her mother and one doctor out of the room and stationed himself by the door to keep them from coming back in, but stood nearby if those left in the room needed him to do anything.

"Probably just over exhaustion mixed with the shock of the good news," reassured the doctor. "A few days' rest will do her well," he added, taking his leave. Allonwë's mother looked relieved.

"I feel awful," her mother said after the doctor had gone. "She tried to tell me she wasn't well. I just thought she didn't want to sit through another 'boring ceremony' like before."

Natanael stepped forward, bowing his head respectfully before addressing the Queen. "Lady Alannah, if I may. I will look after her for tonight and allow you to return to your people to assure them all is well. I will make sure she is well cared for."

The queen turned, her brow still furrowed with worry, nodded and agreed.

"Thank you, Natanael," she added, resting her hand on his

shoulder before reluctantly leaving. She cast one last worried glance back at her daughter, asleep in her bed, before leaving. Natanael turned back and looked at Allonwë's sleeping form. She was beautiful, still, quiet, and peaceful. It was a rare moment for her to be all of those at once. She almost looked like a statue.

So as not to disturb her, Natanael carefully took one of her extra pillows that was falling off the bed, straightened, and looked at her sleeping form one last time before smacking her in the face with it.

"OW!" she exclaimed, muffled by the pillow.

"Get up, we're off schedule," Natanael replied, masking his amusement as he moved to grab her travel bag from the wardrobe and finish packing it for her.

"I fainted in front of hundreds of people, right after getting forcibly betrothed to a childhood friend I have no romantic feelings toward, and the first thing you do when you get me alone in my room is to hit me over the face with a pillow while I'm lying there unconscious?!" demanded Allonwë.

"You're right," replied Natanael, stuffing something into her bag. "You have been reading too many gag-inducing romance novels. Perhaps we should pick up a wider selection on our way back - assuming we live that long. Besides, you weren't unconscious, you were only pretending."

"At least if I die, my fiancé will mourn me!" she retorted.

"Don't have your would-be husband mourning for your death when it hasn't happened yet. The poor boy is probably busy picking out his own funeral garments," replied Natanael, looking about for anything he may have missed.

"It's a wedding, Nana! He's not ending his life!" argued Allonwë, throwing a pillow at him.

"There's a reason the groom's ceremonial wedding garments match closely to his ceremonial burial garments," replied Natanael, grabbing one last thing and stuffing it into the bag.

The door opened to admit Elias and closed quickly after he entered.

"So what is your plan for getting out of-" Elias stopped mid-sentence and stride when he saw Allonwë and Natanael packing her bag. Whistling, he raised his eyebrows in surprise. "More drastic than I expected, but it could work. So, your plan is to elope with your personal bodyguard, of all people? Sounds like a slutty romance novel."

"What?! No!" Natanael and Allonwë exclaimed, making it sound rehearsed. Elias gave them a disbelieving look.

"No, no-no," repeated Allonwë, glaring at both of them. She held out her hands as if trying to stave off an onslaught of questions and accusations

"My plan is much better!"

"Care to explain, then?" asked Elias.

"Explaining will take too long," interjected Natanael, pulling the chord to the bag taut, and moving to the balcony doors. Outside, he dropped the bag into the hollow of the large oak tree growing right beside the railing.

"Then I'll sum it up," quipped Allonwë. She looked at Elias and thought for a moment. "I found a bracelet, nearly got beheaded by a haunted suit of armor, gambled the bracelet away to three random travelers I've never seen before in my life, got back to the castle, found out it was not just a bracelet but an extremely powerful magical weapon, and now I need to get it back before my parents find out... Did I miss anything?" she asked Natanael over her shoulder as he passed by to grab her traveling boots.

"You mean besides the part where you single-handedly doomed us all with a shiny piece of jewelry?" he asked, handing her the travel boots with a casual look. "No, I think you've covered it."

She took the boots from him with a smile. "Just think of

what I could do with a matching necklace and ring set! Oh! And a headpiece! There needs to be a headpiece."

Natanael rolled his eyes, not wanting to imagine the prospects, and moved to grab her sword and scabbard from the mount on the wall. "It's time to move, princess."

"You know," she said, looking at Elias. "If I had to get betrothed, I'm glad it's to someone like you who isn't old and doesn't have really gross, long ears down to his knee caps! At least you help with shenanigans."

"Yeah, about that..." began Elias.

"You're not going to help with the shenanigans?" exclaimed Allonwë, upset.

"No-no-no," he assured her, waving his hand dismissively. "That's fine - I'll make something up." Allonwë looked relieved. "It's just... about this whole betrothal thing... I'd be lying if I said I didn't have feelings for you..." He paused, unsure how to word what he was thinking.

Both Natanael and Allonwë stared at him, also unsure how to word what they were thinking. Where was this coming from? Was Elias going to propose on his own? Natanael wondered. There was a twist in his gut at the idea. But hadn't he been just as surprised as Allonwë had? Or was that shock a mock look of surprise and betrayal? Had he just wanted to ask on his own but their parents' beat him to it?

"But..." he added at last. "They're completely platonic. It would be like marrying my little sister."

"Oh, thank the gods!" Allonwë sat down on the bed rather forcefully in utter relief. Even Natanael looked relieved, having thought Elias was going to ask her to go through with the wedding. "But, I know! It's like - I love you like a brother and all, but family is still family."

"Completely agree. I mean, like you said. Glad it's you over some creepy old elf," agreed Elias. "But even so!"

"Exactly," nodded Allonwë. "There's gotta be a way out of

this. We just need to figure it out. Well, after we get the bracelet back, that is."

"Oh, by all means," Elias nodded. "It'll give me time to explain things to Murna."

"Murna?" Allonwë exclaimed excitedly. "Is that the girl you love?!"

Elias blushed. "Well, I was going to ask for her hand in marriage once she came of age in two weeks, but our parents beat me to the punch."

"Oh, pft - go on and ask her!" Allonwë scoffed. "Forty is way too old to be waiting to get married! We need to take a leaf from the human's book and do that stuff before we're twenty! We'd have babies everywhere! Make this place more interesting!" Elias laughed, but Natanael walked between them and grabbed her by the wrist.

"Sorry to break up this lovely reunion, but we have less than half an hour to get to the northern gate. That's when the guard duty changes. If we miss that window, we may miss our only chance at getting the bracelet back."

He had gone and done some investigation to see which route the travelers had taken once they left. He assumed they had waited for the guard change like he was planning to once they reached the gate in and out of the city. If it weren't aiding their escape tonight, then he would have beefed up the security on it immediately. For now, he had to wait and do something about it when they got back.

If they got back.

"Good luck with Murna!" Allonwë waved goodbye to Elias as they made their way to the balcony, crawled over the railing, and started down the tree.

She loved this tree. It brought shade in the summer, cover from rain or snow, was a great hiding place with its hollow trunk to hide things from her parents or the staff, and made a great escape route for nights like tonight. It was a good, diabolical tree looking all innocent and plant like.

"Oh!" she called back up to Elias. "Don't forget to buy us as much time as you can! Good luck!"

"You too!" called Elias as he waved goodbye and shut the doors.

They reached the ground and made their way to the stables. Earlier that night, Natanael had told the stable boy that so long as he made it back for his morning duties, he could go enjoy himself at the festival tonight. Happily obliging, the boy skipped off, leaving the two of them a clear escape to the royal pastures.

Natanael went to the corner of the back stall and unburied some saddle bags laden with provisions that he had hidden under the freshly laid hay. Tying them in place, and helping Allonwë into her saddle, he led the horses out. From the pastures, they went through the wooden fence marking the boundaries, through the thick woods, waited for the guard change before escaping unnoticed from the city. They avoided any villages that were scattered throughout the hills so as not to leave any obvious trail behind them.

Once past most of the houses, they broke into a gallop and began their long, long journey.

Lesson 4

AND I WOULD HAVE GOTTEN AWAY WITH IT TOO IF IT WEREN'T FOR THAT DAMNED CHICKEN!

The morning found them at the top of an incline overlooking a city in the distance. They would have to dismount from here, but they weren't far from the main road where they could join the general market traffic without attracting attention. One thing he'd have to be careful to do, however, would be to hide his royal armor. Stopping to put on a cloak, Natanael glanced up at Allonwë, who still sat on her horse.

"We'll have to dismount from here, princess. That incline isn't safe to ride down," he instructed.

"Ah-ah!" she tsked. "None of that!"

Natanael furrowed his brow. What was she going on about now?

"You will call me by Allonwë out here," she instructed.

Natanael bit back a sarcastic comment. "And pray tell why this change?" he asked, resisting deliberately putting a 'princess' at the end.

"Who knows who we'll run into out here," she replied as a-matter-of-factly. "There could be thieves, brigands, bandits and, worse!"

Natanael opened his mouth to correct her, but clamped it shut with a sigh.

"And besides," she continued, ignoring the unspoken remark, "if they knew I was a you-know-what, they'd kidnap me and demand a ransom."

For once, Natanael didn't have a good comeback, as much as he wanted to. She was right. If they were going to go low profile, calling her princess for the world to hear would only cause more trouble.

He sighed again. He could feel a headache coming on.

"As you wish."

"As you wiiiish...?" she trailed off, waiting for him to fill in the space with her name.

He rolled his eyes.

"Just get off the horse," he replied, moving forward towards the trail. She grinned, dismounting and following his lead. Using such formal speaking was a step in the right direction and she'd take it.

"How will we know what road they took if we don't follow their trail exactly?" questioned Allonwë. While her initial thrill had subsided and she was regretting not getting at least a little more sleep before she left, she was still too excited to be grumpy.

"While you were off gallivanting about Sitani castle, I was doing some tracking," replied Natanael, who was used to having to stay up for days at a time between Allonwë and his duties. "They took the road north, northeast of us, which ultimately leads to the City of Sils. We took a detour to the nearest town to get provisions for the trip, but as long as we head that general direction, we should get there in a few more days... So long as we don't get sidetracked or lost," he looked at her pointedly. "Once we are there, we'll get a room at the inn, and I'll look around town for any signs of them. You'll stay there and make sure no one steals our stuff."

"Well, that's no fun!" argued Allonwë. "I wanna go with

you! Get in on the action! Not play babysitter to a sack of potatoes."

"No," Natanael said firmly. She wasn't winning this time. "You've been in enough trouble already, Allonwë."

She looked at him, a pout plastered across her face, but didn't argue. Not with that tone. She knew she'd pushed him far enough for one argument.

She sighed. "This is the part of the adventure they always leave out. The boring traveling part. It's supposed to be exciting to go on an adventure! Where are all the bad guys, and witches and wizards, giant towers? I wanna go off sword fighting and rescuing damsels in distress!"

"You are a damsel in distress," muttered Natanael under his breath. "Or rather a damsel that causes distress."

"You'd think there'd be one on every corner from all the books I've read," continued Allonwë, having been too lost in thought to hear him. What kind of adventure would they have? she wondered. Her thoughts strayed back to the heart stone bracelet, and the things she'd read. So, if my personality color was purple, I wonder what color Natanael would be. "Nana," she began curiously.

"Yes, pr-..." he caught himself with a sigh. "Yes, Allonwë?" He had to get used to not calling her princess on this journey. Now she had him paranoid about people finding out who she was and trying to rob her. Or worse.

What if there were thieves in the woods?

"What color personality do you think you have?" she asked.

"...What?" Natanael actually stopped his horse and looked at her.

She repeated the question, the look on her face serious. He stared at her for a full ten seconds as if she'd half lost her mind and he was waiting for her to correct herself. Turning his horse when she said nothing, he shook his head and continued forward.

"Allonwë, you never cease to amaze me in asking the strangest, off the wall questions," he replied.

"I think you'd be silver," she continued, ignoring his statement. "Pure, strong, and bright," she decided with a nod.

"As you wish," he replied.

"Well, aren't you going to ask me what color mine is or where I got the idea for such a question in the first place?" she asked brightly.

"No," replied Natanael flatly.

Allonwë twittered on despite his apparent lack of enthusiasm in the conversation, but Natanael listened as carefully as he watched for thieves and things that could attack them or try to hurt her. Yes, sometimes she exasperated him beyond all reason. Yes, he was teased by all the other soldiers for being the royal babysitter. And sometimes he wished she wouldn't do things that got her into so much trouble.

But at the same time, he was glad to get away from Sitani Castle for a while. No colonel's breathing down his neck, no getting teased for her shenanigans, no worrying about the king or queen walking around the corner and finding her doing something that would horrify them and get them both berated, despite his obvious attempts at trying to stop her.

Why did the castle need such strict regulations, anyway? He understood the military reasons. Those prepared the soldier for real-life situations that could save lives. That he didn't have a problem with. It was how strictly they treated Allonwë. They were so afraid she was going to step one toe out of line that they drilled the rules into her to where they ensured she would find inventive ways to not follow them. Or find loopholes in them to exploit to her advantage. Which she did.

Every day.

Even now, she was enjoying the freedom more than she realized. She never prattled on like this in public at the castle. Only in private, and then still never this free when a maid or some other servant was around. She was smart in knowing they had ears, too. She'd learned that early in childhood, when her parents had used them as extended ears to keep a check on her.

It was nice to hear her let loose with no cares like this. He just didn't exactly know how to respond to it. If she would talk about something he could offer some sort of actual opinion on, he wouldn't mind joining in the conversation, but... What color personality he had? How could you even fathom such a thing? It amazed him, though. The imagination she could have. Even if it got her in trouble.

Often.

A few hours passed, and Allonwë's prattle had settled down a bit as she observed their surroundings with growing interest and listened to the unfamiliar sounds of the forest. She would ask him questions from time to time about different plants, trees, and birds, and for once, he could actually give an answer to her questions. These things he knew about, amongst others. Things that didn't require an untamed imagination to ponder over.

It struck up one of the first normal conversations they'd had in months that didn't involve him trying to convince her not to do something reckless. At least, so far, it hadn't. He was keeping his fingers crossed on that one. The pleasantness of the moment lasted them until nightfall, where they camped beneath the spread of a broad feathery fir tree.

In a few days' time, they'd reached Sils.

"I've paid for a room or one night," Natanael said as he set their bags down, and Allonwë checked out the room. It was a rather pleasant inn for the city, but it was nothing compared to the rooms she was used to in Sitani.

She loved it.

"It feels like we're really roughing it, Nana! This is so exciting!" she chittered happily.

Natanael had to hide his grin. "No, princess, this isn't quite roughing it."

"Ah-ah!" she reminded him. "None of that. Call me by my name, Nana."

"As soon as you call me by mine, princess," countered Natanael.

"Oh, but what fun is that?" she demanded. "You're my Nana, Nana!"

"And you are my princess, my lady," he quipped.

She pouted with him for a moment before sighing heavily and rolling her eyes.

"Oh fine," she consented. "Natanael."

The tone she used was one she normally used to imitate people she found rather stupid.

"Don't say it so weird... *Allonwë*," he said, mimicking her mocking tone hiding a grin with a grimace. He was enjoying this more than he probably should be. She stuck her tongue out at him, but couldn't stop the grin from spreading across her own face. Despite the danger they could be in, the excitement was infectious. Perhaps this was a chance to breathe without worrying about severe backlash.

Getting a few things out of his saddle pack, and slinging a small bag over his shoulder, Natanael instructed Allonwë to stay put and get some rest while he scouted out the city for clues on the travelers' whereabouts or the direction they had gone. She milled about the room for a moment, before pulling back the curtain to watch him leave the inn, making his way down the street.

With a grin and a giggle, she tiptoed over to their bags and grabbed some coins the pouch. Natanael was being silly. Of course, she couldn't just stay in the room and guard some potatoes. She had to get some clothes she wouldn't be recognized in. Being of royal blood had its disadvantages. You didn't get to have peasant clothes to blend in with. You had to make do on your own or just be stared at like you'd grown two arms out the side of your head and were making rude gestures at people.

In all honesty though - why was being of royal blood so astonishing? It wasn't nearly as glamorous as people made it out to be. Too many obligations, parades, and rules. It was ridiculous. And then there was that whole betrothal thing.

Shaking her head, she made her way down the stairs. What a ridiculous notion. Why on earth would they think she'd want to marry Elias? Probably for the same reason they thought behaving like a statue and not learning how to breathe fire was a good thing. Maybe it just reminded them too much of the dragon wars or something.

Dragons were fairly interesting looking creatures though. So many species and kinds. And a lot of them could fly. It would be the most amazing feeling to learn how to fly, though. If she could grow wings, she wanted a set of furry ones. You'd always see scaley or feathered ones, but scaley seemed itchy and cold, and feathers made her sneeze. Fur would shed everywhere and drive her parents insane. It was a beautiful thought. Thye'd never allow her in court covered in fur. Not to mention the horror on their faces if she randomly sprouted flight capable appendages out of her back.

Giggling to herself as she traversed the streets, she noticed a few people giving her strange looks and whispering amongst themselves. A high blood? their confused looks seemed to say. Walking among the commoners? Couldn't be - why would they do such a strange thing? Though she was wearing a rather pretty dress... Much too fine for what they sold in the markets around here. Wasn't there something familiar about her hair and eyes, too?

Ducking into a clothing vendor's tent to avoid the gaze and whispers around her, Allonwë glanced around for anything inconspicuous she could buy to wear. Maybe something brown. Or green. Ick. No... Something that wouldn't clash with her hair and eyes. Possibly something to make Natanael irritably flustered.

Digging through a few things, and getting some help from the merchant, she picked out a striped, sleeveless, sky-blue shirt wrap with gold trim that had a purple belt that settled just below her bust, fastening with a golden button. It fell past her hips, opening in the front to reveal her naval, and was decorated with a golden cord around the high collar. Donning a pair of striped green pants with a wide belt that matched the one on the shirt, she slipped on a pair of thigh-high boots, tying the ensemble together.

No telling what kind of muck they could wade through would be the excuse she gave Natanael for getting them, but really, they were just too cute not to wear with this outfit. And how often did she get to wear such things? Not often enough.

Only in defense classes and riding lessons did she ever get to wear something besides skirts. Her parents would have a fit if they could see her now! Okay, so perhaps it wasn't the most inconspicuous thing she could have chosen, but damn, she looked good!

She observed her form in the mirror, happily, before moving to her old garments and going through her pockets for some money to pay for her things. Unfortunately, despite how much she searched, the coins she'd taken before she left were nowhere to be found. She checked the clothes she was wearing and tore through the old ones several more times before she could admit she might have been robbed at some point.

Wondering how she would explain this to the merchant, and even worse, Natanael, she briefly wondered if she could just exchange her old gown for the new items. Goodness knows it was expensive enough.

"It wasn't hard. We tricked her into making a bet she couldn't win and she handed it over," a familiar voice reached Allonwë's ears, distracting her from her momentary crisis.

"We needed her too, idiots!" came the reply. "Go back and find her. Here's a location spell in case they've moved her."

They needed her? What did they need her for? Poking her head out the back of the tent to look around, she saw several people walking by, many crates of live chickens, a few dogs scavenging for food, and off to one side, the lead traveler that had taken the bracelet, arguing with someone she couldn't see for shadows and cloaks. In fact, the figure was hard to focus on. As if the light were moving away from them to better hide them.

Typical, she thought ruefully, scrunching up her nose. The one time she had the chance to have a cloak that glorious and someone had pickpocketed her. Blending into the shadows that well in the middle of the day took talent. And a well-designed garment. She wanted to be a cape veiled vigilante too!

Stepping out of the back of the tent to get a better look at the stranger, Allonwë was greeted with a low, angry warning cackle from a rooster loose near the corner. Standing up and bobbing its head towards her, the rooster clucked, then let out a long warning cackle again.

"Shhh," she warned quietly, shooing it away. "I can't hear!"

Glancing back up, however, she noticed the traveler and the cloaked figure moving away from her. Quickly trying to move to get closer to see where they were headed, the rooster crowed and attacked her ankles violently, surprising Allonwë, who shrieked and began high stepping and stumbling to get away from the creature.

Becoming more irritated the further out in the street she danced, the rooster pecked, scratched, and beat with his wings as if trying to keep her from going anywhere, only making things worse. The folds of the tent moved back to reveal a surprised-looking merchant, who scowled and pointed at Allonwë declaring her a thief, and all eyes that weren't already watching her turned to see what the commotion was about.

The rooster, as if given new purpose, managed to fly up a foot or so to attack her knees before moving back down to her feet.

Down the row of tents, a couple of guards exchanged looks, wandering towards the tumult. When they cleared the crowd enough to see what was going on, Allonwë kicked the rooster loose from her leg and right into the guard's face. Realization hit the red-headed princess faster than those around her and she turned on heel, running for her life.

The guard hissed angrily, throwing the rooster back at her before thinking of his actions and the fowl flapped its wings, its air-born vengeance reigning down on the poor girl, sending her tumbling into another tent and tripping over a table. She and the contents tumbled to the ground, an oil lamp included, and the metal can clattered across the floor, setting the liquid contents - which had splashed everywhere - on fire.

Finally separated from the foul creature long enough to stand and get her bearings, Allonwë looked around in horror. How was it she always managed to set things on fire? Every. Single. Time. She searched for something - anything - to put out the fire, but her thoughts were too scattered to think as the blasted attack bird set in on her yet again.

Grabbing a nearby crate, she held it off as her eyes searched for aid. There were cooking utensils here and there, some cloth, and sacks of vegetables and - Aha! Flour! Grabbing a bag, she ripped it open, slinging its contents across the tent, dousing the chicken, the fire, and the two guards that emerged into the tent after her. Staring wide eyed at the scene, Allonwë picked up the rooster, throwing it back at the guards and fled past the screaming merchant who'd come in to see what on earth had crashed into the back of her tent.

High tailing it out of the front of the tent and through the streets, Allonwë made her way out of the marketplace and back towards the inn where Natanael was emerging, looking rather stressed and irritated. When his eyes fell on Allonwë running straight for him, he barely had time to register a look of confusion before she rushed past him, grabbing his arm and hauling him alongside her. A roar of anger sounded behind them, but Allonwë wouldn't let him turn back long enough to see what it was.

"Why are we running?!" he demanded as they ducked into an alleyway to lose their pursuers. They were taking several many turns, soon talking between gasps for breath.

"Remember when you told me to stay put and watch our things?" she called back over her shoulder, trying to breathe past the stitch in her side.

"Yes?" he shouted back.

"I didn't listen," she informed him.

"I gathered that - what are you running from?!" he called, trying to catch up with her.

Damn, she could run when motivated. And apparently she was very, very well motivated. Getting her to do this back at Sitani was like trying to teach a horse how to paint pictures. What had she gotten herself into now? Probably set something else on fire. He just hoped it wasn't someone important this time. Like the town's priest or something.

"That damn chicken!" she answered, skidding to a stop, nearly making Natanael smack into her. "There!" she hissed, pointing ahead of her as she ducked behind a doorway. She yanked her bodyguard inside as well and peeked around. There, exiting a pub, were the two figures from before.

"Chicken?" he asked, looking too. She was running from a chicken? When he spotted the two figures, he tensed. The one in the brown garb was the traveler they'd bartered the bracelet off to. And by the looks of it, he was making another trade. The figure he was with was hard to make out, but he could tell they were military and possibly female. If it was a female, she carried herself well, making Natanael wonder if they really could handle this on their own.

"Those two started this whole mess," Allonwë muttered under her breath.

"They saw you?" he hissed. Of all the things she could have possibly done in his absence, setting a priest on fire looked to be the least troubling at the moment. Allonwë shook her head, only mildly relieving him.

"No, I went to buy myself a change of clothes so I could go unnoticed," she said. "I mean, walking around in a princess dress will get me more stares than running around naked."

"That actually started out as a very intelligent thing to do," he thought out loud.

"Why do you sound surprised?" she hissed back. "And what do you mean started?"

"How did they start this mess if they didn't see you?" he countered, avoiding the questions.

"Well, at first I was shopping for this outfit, but I couldn't find anything that really caught my eye," she began, even though the point had been to blend in.

"Allonwë to the point," Natanael cut in, though she barreled on, ignoring him.

"But then I found these - and they were just too adorable not to get - so I took them in the back to try them on, only I realized someone had pickpocketed me. And I just knew he was going to think I was trying to steal them, but really I wasn't Nana, I'm a victim too! But then I heard this voice out the back of the tent and when I poked my head out to investigate, this diabolically feathered demon from the pits of destruction attacked me out of nowhere! Then the merchant started calling me rude names that were completely unnecessary and sent these troll-sized men after me to do who knows what, and then there was fire everywhere and flour and that ridiculous watch bird attacked me again - and do you know it pecked me on the head? If I ever see another one of those foul misanthropic creatures again, it better be on a skewer!"

"Someone has pickpocketed you. You stole these clothes, and set someone's tent on fire," Natanael shortened, pinching the bridge of his nose again.

The list of things they were going to have to correct and repair before all hell broke loose was getting bigger. Meanwhile, they were still trying to clean up their original mess.

Looking past her again, he watched the two exchange a case for something small, wrapped in a cloth. By the looks of it, it could very well have been the bracelet they were searching for. And if they were making a shady deal in the middle of a market where no one would think twice about the exchange, it could mean anything. Who knew if they understood just exactly what they had or not? If they didn't, it would be hell to get it back without explaining it. If they did...?

They were probably in over their heads. But what more could they do? They couldn't go to Sitani with this. He'd be fired on the spot. Imprisoned. Maybe sentenced to death if he was lucky and not considered a traitor to the crown. As it was, he wasn't entirely sure how they would keep them from doing just that anyway when they returned from this misadventure.

"And I found our culprits," Allonwë added in a whisper, watching them as well. "I don't like the looks of that guy." She nodded towards the figure, examining the object beneath the cloth. It was too far away to see from where they stood, but they were apparently satisfied, pocketing it before saying something more to the traveler. With a nod, they parted ways, and Natanael's heart sank.

Which one should they follow? On the one hand, if they traded the bracelet, they didn't need to follow the wayward traveler any longer, but that presented additional problems with their new target. Just who were they and what did they want with it? If it was just a piece of jewelry, they could offer to buy it, but what did they have besides their word that they could hold up such an agreement? If they knew it was a weapon and wanted to use it, how could they go up against it if the tales were true?

If they followed the stranger and the traveler still had it, they could waste valuable time trying to recover the ground lost and there was no guarantee that they'd find them once more. Or at least before they sold it to someone else in the meantime.

"There's something that's been bothering me," he voiced out loud. "I see the leader. But I haven't seen heads or tails of the other two since our encounter back on castle grounds." He scratched his chin, surveying the area. "Did you see them when you-?" he began, but did a double take. "Allonwë?" he asked, turning a circle. He caught sight of her red hair disappearing around a corner in the direction the stranger went, and cursed, scrambling after her. He needed to retire a few centuries early, he decided.

Ducking around tents and into alleys between more permanent fixtures, Natanael struggled to keep up, catching sight of her hair or figure disappearing around one corner or the next, through a crowd or past a booth. How was she getting so far away so quickly? he wondered. Turning down another street, he came to a screeching halt as the other two travelers he'd been worrying about stood side by side with their leader.

Allonwë was nowhere in sight.

"Found you," he said, spreading his arms and looking to his companions, whose grins mimicked his own. "Thank you for saving us the trouble of tracking you back down. Seems like we made a mistake and we need that little lady friend of yours, too.

"Where is she?" Natanael demanded, his training kicking in and setting him on edge.

"Oh, we're taking care of her, don't you worry."

"You came for the bracelet on purpose, didn't you?" Natanael stated. "That was no mere accident. You tricked us."

"Oh, he's a sharp one," mocked the lead.

Natanael drew back his cloak and drew his sword.

"Then again, perhaps I spoke too soon," he added, drawing back his hood. The traveler's skin darkened to a grey, his smile spreading across his face, which seemed to grow and contort in size. Claws protruded from under the edges of the cloak, and a serpentine tail slipped out the back. Untying the knot at his throat, the traveler threw back his cloak. His mouth growing large enough to swallow Natanael whole, and the scaled skin that stretched across the dis-proportioned body seemed dry in the heat. As if ready to shed and form a new surface, sleek and smooth. The maw parted in a feral hiss that sent a shiver down Natanael's spine. The stench that rolled off the creature was nauseating. Four days dead with a fresh coat of decay.

"Nagas?" Natanael breathed, feeling like the realization had knocked the wind out of him. Snake creatures that could take on the form of a person and go disguised in public. Since when did they stray into these parts? And since when did they smell like death?

"Naga," the creature corrected. "My companions have other things in store for you. Should you live that long."

Natanael barely had time to register the movement before the Naga's tail caught him in the stomach and slammed him against the wall. The air was forced from his lungs, the back of his skull greeting the brick and mortar like old enemies clashing. Allonwë's retreating form flashed before his eyes and he wondered if it hadn't been an illusion cast to lure him there. And if it had been where the real Allonwë had gone. Was she safe? She'd probably be cheering for him to fight back right about now if she were near. He hit the ground on his hands and knees and was promptly met with a blow to the back.

The world narrowed. The tiny alleyway seemed to be all that was left in the world. There were no sounds. No other people. No smells or sights or tastes other than fresh blood, the feel of the cobbled street beneath his fingertips, and more blood in the back of his throat. Black spots appeared in his sight, and he was brutally aware of his inability to form a coherent thought other than, 'Am I to die here?'

He didn't want to. And for a moment, that thought allowed him to regain a bit of himself. The taste of blood in his mouth made him wonder if he'd bitten his tongue or if he had internal bleeding. There wasn't anything on him that didn't hurt right now and it was too hard to breathe with the air refusing to come back into his lungs. His head was swimming. Movements were sluggish. His vision wanting to blur. He'd been right about this crew. They were not to be messed with.

But he couldn't let them go. He couldn't let this end here. They may have had Allonwë, and he was her only protection. Her only safe passage back to the palace. He had allowed her to come this far, and he was responsible should anything happen to her. The only thing standing in his way was this trio.

While Natanael didn't fight unnecessarily, he had never backed down from his duties.

Finding the strength to stand again was no easy task. But the surprise that came when he found his bearings and didn't immediately get knocked back down by his opponent was enough to make him stumble upright. Grabbing his sword, he faced the trio who'd turned to leave and took a breath. The black spots in his vision faded and instantly his head felt clearer. Doubling over, he coughed, retching up a bit of blood in the process. Oh, he definitely had some internal bleeding.

But he could breathe. And he could think. The world was no longer confined to this tiny cobbled street anymore. He could hear the crowds, smell the fresh baked goods, and feel the air in his lungs again like a cool crisp breeze on a hot summer day. He looked up from beneath his brow to see the trio had stopped to look at him dubiously.

"Why d'ya get up?" the Naga complained. "Now I have to waste time killin' ya."

"Don't touch my Nana!" The Naga roared as something leapt onto its back, throwing something over its head so it couldn't see.

Natanael blinked, dumbstruck, as he watched Allonwë ride on the shoulders of this bulbous creature, trying to wrap her arms around its neck. Was she seriously trying to strangle it?

"What are you doing?" he shouted. Had she lost her mind? What possessed her to jump into this fight after watching him get his ass handed to him?

"Saving you!" she bristled, as if it should have been obvious.

"Have you lost your mind?" he asked, though he already knew the answer. Allonwë tied the cloth around the creature's neck so it couldn't remove it from its face, just as it grabbed her and tossed her at Natanael, who caught her before tumbling to the ground with a strained grunt. The creature instantly shrank back down to its human size as Natanael and Allonwë scrambled to their feet.

"Sword it!" she screamed, gesturing wildly and trying to get him to respond. Natanael's eyes lit up as he understood, and dove for the creature as it grappled with the cloak. Pulling the cover from its eyes, it snarled at Natanael just before he impaled it through the chest. Face to face with the traveler that had caused them so much trouble, he watched the life fade from its eyes, its skin turning the same deathly grey. Natanael pulled back, shocked, as it melted before him like waxy sludge from a rapidly heated candle.

The pile of grey mud that used to be the traveler settled between the two elves and the two remaining travelers. All eyes strayed from it to their opponents. Natanael wondered if they would attack or run. Perhaps if he stood his ground, they would lose their nerve.

"Who wants to die next?" he asked, twirling his sword. The others exchanged looks, frowning.

"We weren't told what to do if they found out," the one on the left said.

"No witnesses," answered the other.

"Should we wait or take care of them now?" the first asked.

Allonwë and Natanael exchanged looks.

Found out what? The look seemed to ask.

Convince them to wait, Allonwë begged silently.

"Wait," the one on the right replied.

"Wait for what?" Natanael asked as he stood between Allonwë and the strange mud. He backed away slowly, sword at the ready.

Before them, the mud began to boil, and the travelers watched it without expression. It undulated and grew like a fountain of lava and formed into a shape, hardening and growing again until the Naga stood before them, unscathed. Allonwë's eyes widened, hair standing on end and heart slamming against her chest as a passage from the books she'd read came to mind:

The Mages of Barlow used the Spell of Asai to arm their best soldiers against an archmage and necromancer.

"You're becoming more of a problem than you're worth," the Naga growled, straightening.

Lesson 5

THE PLOT CHICKENS

Natanael gripped his sword tighter, angling himself between the Naga and Allonwë. These weren't normal creatures. Nagas weren't immortal - they were not capable of being impaled with a sword and surviving. Nagas didn't melt into smelly mud puddles when impaled by said sword, only to reform like a Golem and be royally angry about it.

Well, the temper part was accurate. Nagas were well known for their tempers. But they most certainly were not known for anything remotely resembling immortality. Or for smelling like death trying to strangle the life out of a rotting corpse. It was as if the smell had become doubly worse, and it was all the elves could do to keep their breakfast down. They tried covering their noses and mouths; the stench making their eyes water.

"What are you?" Natanael demanded.

He made an assessment of his injuries and while he was severely bruised and cut up, his head and jaw pounding like a white-hot fire in his skull, the armor he wore under the traveling cloak had taken the brunt of the force behind the blows. He didn't think he had any cracked or broken bones - yet.

Though, if he stuck around, that was bound to change rather quickly. He briefly wondered if he could make an escape, but worried if they could hide the other things besides the stench of death and a full-sized Naga under their cloaks. There was no telling what kind of other creatures were flanking their current opponent.

He glanced around, looking for something they could use a distraction. An item, a passerby - anything - but the streets were bare of anything useful, and there were no people in sight. In fact, he realized, there was not even the sound of a bustling market.

There was a complete and utter silence around them. No birds, no click-clacking of horse hooves on the cobblestone, no merchants calling out sales and goods at the top of their lungs, or a breeze to stir the dust of the surrounding streets. No witnesses to see or hear the brawl or aid them from certain death.

If nothing - no sound or creature - could get in this bubble of silence, would they even be capable of escaping it? Natanael's own panic rose, but he fought it back vehemently. No good would come if he were to panic now. It would only ensure they wouldn't get out alive.

"Necromancy," he heard Allonwë breathe.

Natanael blinked. Necromancy? His skin crawled as he looked at the three travelers in a new light. That would explain the stench. That would explain the inability to kill them by skewering them. But it didn't quite explain why the Naga turned into a pool of thick, tar-like liquid before forming and retaking its shape. There was something more going on here, but he wasn't sure they'd have the time to get to the bottom of it and still make it out alive. His chief concern was strictly survival.

"What did your study say about how not to be killed by the undead?" Natanael whispered back.

Allonwë racked her brains to remember anything that

could help them in their current predicament, but every spell they had taught her or that she read up on required spell work and ingredients they did not have the time to make or have access to at the moment.

Her eyes darted around as she tried to unscramble her thoughts. Why didn't anyone ever invent practical magic one could use on the spur of the moment? What use was it knowing a plethora of spells if you couldn't use them in a moment of crisis? Then again, she surmised, her teachers had probably avoided teaching her practical magic out of fear she'd get herself killed or, worse, turn it against them. Perhaps she hadn't quite thought her retaliation phase through.

"You have two options here," the Naga was saying, its slit pupils constricting in the light now that it was free of the hood and cloak it had been wearing.

"That's generous," Allonwë quipped, but couldn't squelch the terrified whimper in her voice.

"You can die peacefully," he replied. "Or we can do this the hard way, and you still die."

"Funny," Natanael replied, taking a slow step back, and raising his sword higher. "I was going to say the same thing to you."

"I like option three," Allonwë squeaked. "You let us leave because we asked nicely."

Why, oh why, did she have to be pick-pocketed at a time like this? She could have bribed them again! Well, to be fair, she had lost a bet during that first encounter, but she would have bribed them now in a heartbeat. If she hadn't been pick-pocketed, chased by a feathered demon, and trapped by these walking sewer pots, she might be working in her new boots by chasing down the person who currently held the bracelet.

"Don't worry, lass," the Naga replied. "It's not you we'll be killin', just your little guardsman."

Both Allonwë and Natanael froze.

"Your plan was to separate us and take her," Natanael guessed.

"Don't be too smart for yourself there," the Naga hissed mockingly. "Wouldn't want to give yer little princess there too much information or we'll be killin' her too."

"Don't touch her!"

"Don't touch him!"

The elves yelled at the same time, scowling.

The Naga laughed.

"Well, aren't you quite the pair," he mused, but the two elves realized this was no longer about accidentally losing a bracelet that just so happen to be a weapon of mass destruction. These people knew exactly who she was and exactly what they were doing.

Allonwë knew there was no chance she would let herself be caught - dead or undead - by this creepy, scaley Naga, and whatever the other two creatures were, standing between them and freedom.

And a breath of fresh air, she thought, nearly gagging again. The smell wasn't one of those scents you could become nose blind to - this was one of those scents that you would gladly give up ever smelling again if it meant never subjecting your nostrils to such a horrifying displeasure.

If only there was a breeze to alleviate the stench. But no. There was no breeze, no people, no sound but their own racing heartbeats, and the clucking of that utterly ridiculous chicken that had chased her halfway across the market.

Clucking...?

Doing a double-take, Allonwë followed the sound of the clucking until her eyes fell behind the travelers, and spotted the feathered hell-spawn that had dogged her every step since that blasted clothing merchant's tent, pecking around suspiciously.

"You'll have to go through me before you ever lay a hand on her!" Natanael snarled.

And while Allonwë appreciated the sentiment behind the statement, she was more worried that the bravado of his words was going to get them killed - or worse, have him turned into an undead Naga too.

She wasn't sure if they could turn him into a Naga, but it certainly was the most unpleasant mental image she'd ever had of Natanael, and never cared to see it come true. Could people be changed into other species? The thought terrified her, but at the same time, if she could choose to be another creature, she'd choose something that could breathe fire. Like a gnome or something. At least then she could get them out of this situation.

"That won't be a problem," the lead traveler replied.

An idea struck Allonwë. Cupping her hands over her mouth, she started heckling them.

"You're no match for my Nana!" she called before doing something completely ridiculous.

She started clucking loudly, flailing around and pretending to flap her arms as if they were wings. If she could get the attention of the chicken, it would come running towards her and she could throw it in the face of the Naga and help them escape.

But the commotion was so utterly ridiculous, that it was enough to distract everyone in the vicinity, including Natanael who stared at her wondering if she had finally lost her mind.

"That's right! I'm calling you a flightless feathered fowl sent from the depths of hell to torture random passersby! You are tiny, annoying, and good for nothing but roasting and devouring! BrockBOK!" she clucked a little more shrilly, catching the attention of the chicken whose head darted up, looking in their direction before letting out what Allonwë could only describe as a war cry. The creature ran straight for them, making her heart leap into her throat. Oh, how she hated that chicken.

The look of shock at the sudden sound splashed across the

Naga's grotesque features, disrupting his calm, collected demeanor. Letting out a feral hiss, he turned to see the chicken running towards them and skittered out of the way. The bird launched itself aiming directly at the face of Allonwë, who screamed, catching the feathered beast midair. The chicken half crowed back in response as it beat its wings against her, frustrated at not being able to get closer.

Allonwë, who was still screaming, started spinning in a circle to add more force behind her throw as she launched it back at the Naga, hitting it square in the face. As the Naga hissed and slapped at the creature, pecking and beating its wings against his face, Allonwë grabbed Natanael's wrist and dragged him away, running as fast as they could away from the travelers.

She took turn after turn, heading back the way they came. There was a street she started to go down, but it made every nerve in her body stand on end. They almost toppled over one another, trying to backpedal and avoid it. She could hear the sounds of the Naga and his companions hissing curses and screaming behind her and the panic was beginning to rise.

The undead were not far behind, and the two elves were running out of options to take. She stopped at a four-way cross street, turning to look in each direction. She focused on each path, hearing the travelers get closer with every step, unable to pinpoint which direction they were coming from.

"We're getting nowhere," Natanael cursed. "We'll just have to face them."

"Or we can get on a roof and see which way to go!" Allonwë replied. "You face them and they'll kill you!"

"There's no way to get to the rooftops from here. It doesn't make any sense! There are no ladders, no doorways. It's like everything is a wall with a window too high to climb into and every street we take leads us back here!" Natanael replied.

There was nothing but sandstone-colored walls

surrounding them, broken up by the occasional window and red curved shingles. The cobbled streets beneath their feet were so uniform with their other surroundings it was surreal and almost didn't appear to be the same city. It was confining and confusing, and Allonwë could see the worry in his eyes beginning to twist into panic. They had taken three streets already and there was no way out.

She looked around them again, chest heaving after running. If her nerves would just stop screaming for one minute and let her think, she could find a way out of this. They'd gone down the north street, they'd gone west and east. But every time she thought of going towards the south street, she could hear their screaming get louder and knew they were heading towards the danger by going that way. Yet thrice now she had avoided it because thrice the voices of their pursuers had been down that way. She took a few steps towards it; the voices getting louder and her nerves were standing on end. She wanted to turn and run, but something stopped her.

"Allonwë! We have to go. They're getting closer!" Natanael called.

"This way!" she yelled back, running down the south street.

"What are you doing?" he shouted after her. "They are coming from that direction!"

"I know!" she called back.

Swearing, Natanael ran after her. The further down the street they went the more fear seemed to warp their senses. They could feel their hearts pulsing and were suddenly very aware of the blood rushing through their veins. Their limbs grew weak, ready to collapse both from the exertion and the sheer dread that coursed through every nerve in their body the further down the street they ran.

The echoes of their feet clattering on the cobbled streets and the angry voices chasing them grew louder and louder, as if the very breath of their pursuers were on their necks. Panic heightened, constricting their throats and preventing them from turning and looking, only running forward faster.

The sounds filled their ears until it was deafening, and Allonwë wanted to cry. She choked on a sob caught in her throat as the air shifted and changed, making it feel as though they were running through water. Everything felt off. Displaced. Wrong. Slow. Misaligned. The sound distorted. The air was so thick around them it was as if it swaddled them in thick sheets of material they couldn't shake off or break free from. Claustrophobia threatened to overtake them.

Then, just as suddenly as they had entered this field of strange atmosphere, they shot out of it like an arrow from a bow and back into the marketplace they had previously disappeared from.

The voices of their pursuers were suddenly changed into the sound of the market. It had been a hunch she wanted to test - to see if it was a spell set up to make them want to avoid the only way out until they could be pinned down. And when it proved true, her heart nearly leapt out of her chest gratefully.

Allonwë gasped, taking in the fresh, cool air around them. It was like she hadn't been able to breathe the entire time she was in there and her lungs ached to taste the crisp air once again. She coughed and gasped and let the tears run down her face freely. She wanted to scrub her skin free of that feeling and never experience it again. Shuddering to herself, the bustle and mismatched tents and buildings surrounding them helping the fear ebb away little by little.

"I don't want to stay here overnight anymore," she told Natanael as she wrapped her arms around herself for warmth even though she was drenched in sweat. "Let's go back to the inn, get our stuff and go."

"We can't," Natanael replied. "They know your face. They

know who you are. Not only are you wanted for stealing those clothes, those creatures will no doubt be waiting for us back at the inn. We have to continue on foot from here on out." He took a few deep breaths, trying to slow his pulse. "But you're right. We can't stay here. We have to keep moving."

She gave a nod. He was right. Of course he was right - he usually was. But that didn't make her feel any better. All their provisions were in there. Their food. The last bit of money they'd brought with them. Their change of clothes. Horses. All of it. The fear she felt back on the south street seemed to trickle its way down her spine. How would they survive without food or money? she wondered silently.

"The safest thing now is going to be getting you back to Sitani Castle in one piece," Natanael replied.

"We can't just give up now!" Allonwë argued.

"We don't know where the bracelet is. There's a necromancer sending undead things to chase you down and kidnap you - which that alone should be disconcerting enough. But on top of that, I just got my ass handed to me by a mutant Naga that doesn't seem too phased when I put a sword through his middle, and there is an unknown enemy out there right now with a weapon that we know nothing about, that we just kindly handed over like a bouquet to some lucky bride! What is there left that we can do, Allonwë? We have to come forward with this so someone with better resources can handle it without putting your life in danger!" he said.

"Well, lucky for you while you chased the glimmer spell look alike of me," Allonwë retorted. "I was finding out which direction the person who has the bracelet now is going. So, if you want to go back to Sitani Castle empty handed, by all means, but I'm going after the bracelet!"

Natanael opened his mouth to reply, but hesitated. "You found out which way they're going?" he repeated, not quite believing he'd heard her correctly.

"Yes," she responded, crossing her arms again and preparing to defend herself in another argument. She had a plethora of arguments ready to be fired off.

"That's..." he began hesitantly. "Actually... that's good," he finished dumbfounded.

He hadn't expected her to do something that would benefit them in this predicament, but so far, she'd done it thrice now.

Allonwë blinked, surprised. "Y... You're not arguing with me?"

"We came all this way to get that shiny piece of dwarf dung," he replied. "I kind of want to finish this quest." In all honesty he had too much riding on this to give up now. He'd just been certain they'd lost any lead they had and was grasping at straws to hold on to hope.

Allonwë beamed at him. Quest. She quite like the sound of that. Every hero had to face trials. And they'd just survived their first! Or was it the second? Did deranged chickens count as a trial?

"Okay then," he said, interrupting her thoughts. "Which way?" he asked.

Allonwë put one hand on her hip, planted her feet and pointed directly in front of her. "East!" she declared firmly, smile plastered across her lips.

"That's north," Natanael replied. She turned a quarter circle to her right towards Natanael and planted her feet again.

"East!" she nodded firmly again as if that's what she'd intended to do all along and hadn't just pointed in the wrong direction entirely.

Natanael had to give it to her; she always went forward with full confidence, even when she was wrong, and corrected it with the same amount of confidence without apology. He let out a laugh and shook his head, beginning the trek towards the outskirts of the city towards the east. It was a humorless laugh but his spirits were lifting just a bit. She skipped after him, smiling happily.

Allonwë and Natanael on a quest to find the bracelet of mass destruction. Her absolute favorite tag team. Partners in crime.

"Oh, I just thought of a way we can get some lunch," Allonwë grinned.

"We're not stealing anything," Natanael replied without skipping a beat.

"But Naaannaaaaaa," she whined. "We don't have any money! How are we supposed to eaaaat?"

"I can hunt, Allonwë," he reminded her flatly.

"Oh," she replied. "OH, you should shoot a bear! Then I can walk around in a bearskin and make everyone think I am a bear elf hybrid with-"

"No," he interrupted.

"Oh, or maybe a deer!" she mused, unperturbed by his denial. "You could cut off its antlers and I can attach them to my head-"

"No," he cut in again.

"What about a-" she continued.

"No," he sighed, rubbing his face.

"But it would make a fantastic crown!" she argued.

"Allonwë you already have a crown," he replied.

"Yeah," she admitted, making grand gestures with her arms as she continued. "but we would cover this one in blood and terrify all who-"

"No," Natanael replied.

"Oh you know what?" Allonwë brightened.

"I'm not wearing one either," he headed her off. He already knew where this was heading. Even if it was just to get her mind off of what they just experienced, he wasn't going to entertain this idea.

"But you would look adorable!" she countered. "We could

make it all cool and bloody and then you could decorate your hair with flowers-"

"No," he replied.

"It'll be great!" she chirped.

"Still no."

Lesson 6

SOMETIMES THERE'S ONLY ONE BED

"This is it," Allonwë's voice broke the silence between them shakily. She fell to her knees, exhaustion overtaking her. "This is my life now."

She propped up on her hands and hung her head. This was the worst part of the journey yet. Not having horses was really becoming much more of a hassle than an adventure. How did people do this all the time? Walk from city to city as if it were nothing? She was pretty certain that her blisters had blisters at this point. There was nothing on her that wasn't aching with the effort to keep pressing on.

"I have climbed upon this hill... and now I will die upon it."

Nana looked back at her over his shoulder and did a double take, rolling his eyes. "Allonwë get up. We've only been walking for twenty minutes. We can still see the city walls."

"Lies!" Allonwë cried, rolling onto her back and staring up at the sky. "Can't we stop and take a break? I feel like we've been walking for days."

"Not unless you're hiding another chicken somewhere in that outfit. I'm pretty sure once those travelers realize what direction we went, they'll be hot on our trail," Nana replied, scanning the tree line ahead of them. "Unless you'd like to stay here and wait on them?"

Allonwë popped up beside him, bits of grass in her hair. "East. East it is."

Her stomach growled loud enough for both of them to hear and she tried to look anywhere but at him. Natanael gave her a look as a small silence stretched between them. Not the first since leaving the city. She could tell she was testing his patience, but honestly, she was just having a hard time admitting she may have gotten them in over their heads. She was experiencing something that she'd never quite experienced before - at least, not on this same level.

Fear.

She'd been afraid before. She'd been terrified. But this was a new kind of fear. The kind of fear that settles in slowly in the back of the mind and eats away at you until it consumes your thoughts. She'd had small scares. She'd been afraid of things. Of people. Things jumping out at her. Surprises that she wasn't expecting. Being afraid of joining the courts not just because she thought she'd be bored to death, but because they would force her to make enormous decisions about other people's lives that she didn't think she was ready to take on as a leader.

But never a gnawing fear that kept her constantly looking over her shoulder, wondering if they were going to survive the night or die from a number of things that had stacked up against them: enemies, lack of food, exhaustion... odds.

"That's what I thought." Natanael sighed as he continued walking, glancing back to make sure she was following.

The frustration he felt was a driving force. The sooner they got the bracelet back, the sooner she would be safe again. But everything was slowly spiraling out of control... and that had him worried. How was he going to keep her from harm? Had that damned chicken not shown up... he didn't want to think about it.

This girl had the most impeccable luck he'd ever seen, but there was no way they could rely on that to get them out of everything. There was no guarantee that if they kept going that they wouldn't get into something they couldn't get themselves out of again.

If the Naga was trading with that hooded figure, were they just as powerful? He was so unfairly mismatched in power and skill with the Naga; he was almost terrified to consider what - or who - was beneath the cloak of the person who now carried the bracelet. What if they were just as bad or worse?

How on earth were they going to get it back if they were no match for the enemies that stood against them? Natanael picked it apart in his mind until he could literally feel the weight of his stress settling on his shoulders and causing him to bend beneath the pressure. Even his own breath was becoming labored and his forehead was beginning to ache from the knot in his brow that refused to be soothed.

"We've been walking for hours." Allonwë whined, though Natanael had to admit she had a point. It was getting dark, and he hadn't realized just how long they'd been traveling. "Can we make camp yet?"

"No," came the reply.

Allonwë opened her mouth to complain, but paused. She exchanged looks with Natanael, who looked just as confused. Neither of them had spoken. The voice had come from up ahead. Coming around the corner of a boulder the size of a small shack, they stumbled across a fair-haired figure sitting cross-legged on another large rock, just big enough to make a seat.

He was an elf, that was certain. The ears gave it away more than anything else. The tips of his ears were probably a good foot and a half long, and the look on Allonwë's face was pure horror.

The older an elf got, the longer the tips of their ears would get. The longest ears she'd ever seen were of the elders of

Sitani's court. Probably a good hand span length. Nothing this ridiculous. Or terrifying.

Before them was probably one of the oldest elves left in existence. Being immortal, elves didn't age the same way as other races, and couldn't be killed by normal processes like disease or old age. But they could be injured beyond saving, starve to death, or the like. It was even hard to poison an elf, and it had to be under certain circumstances for the poison to even be remotely effective at all. An elf had to already be on their last leg for the poison to kill them. The only reason there weren't more elves this old walking around was because most of them were killed off in the Great Elf and Dragon Wars.

The elder before them sat calmly amongst the trees and the bramble as if he were slowly becoming one with his surroundings. His eyes were solid white, his hands poised in his lap as he meditated, and his hair fell about his shoulders, his clothes as old and tattered as he looked.

"Hello there," Natanael called, only to be hushed by Allonwë. "What?" he asked. "I'm offering greetings."

"We don't know who he is - what if he's with those you know what's?" Allonwë hissed.

"I can hear you," the meditating elf called, not shifting from his position as if he were a talking stone.

Allonwë wasn't even sure if he was breathing.

"Apologies," Natanael called. "We were just looking for a place to set up camp. We've been traveling all day, and have been in a bit of a hurry."

"As I can see, it's not my problem," came the stiff reply.

"Never said it was," Allonwë retorted.

There was a small silence as the elf seemed to blink for the first time since their meeting, and pupils came into view. He glanced at them, steely eyed and blank faced, as he glanced over at them.

"You're still here," he surmised.

"You're somewhat perceptive," Allonwë replied, earning a smack from Natanael.

"What we mean to say is-" Natanael began, trying to retain at least a little common decency, but the elf cut him off.

"You may not stay here. This is my rock. This is my meditation spot. Go away," he dismissed as if that were the end of it.

"Well, we're not going to stay on your rock. We're going to stay on the ground near the rock as this patch of land right here doesn't belong to you, it belongs to the common traveler," Allonwë quipped, hoping her bluff would work enough to annoy this elf as much as he had annoyed her.

His eyes snapped back to her and for a moment, the combination of blonde hair and blue eyes was the most chilling and terrifying sight she'd ever seen. It well convinced her he could murder her right then and there and feel no remorse whatsoever. Allonwë swallowed hard and tried to retain her false sense of self confidence.

"No, it doesn't!" the elf replied indignantly.

"Does too," Allonwë replied.

"Not!" the elf argued, obviously not used to this sort of response.

"Is too!" Allonwë argued, too stubborn to let it go now.

Natanael was at a loss for words as he watched this old man argue with Allonwë as if they were both five-year-olds. The elder elf stood and stomped his foot irritably.

"It! Is! Not!" he all but whined.

"Prove it!" Allonwë countered. "Where's the documents stating that you own this area and its surrounding foliage? If what you say is true and you have proper documentation, we will leave the premises and you can go back to your creepy staring contest with the trees!"

While her argument would have never held up in court, Natanael acknowledged, it was apparently doing a damn good job at the moment with this stranger who seemed to be just as looney as she was. When he hesitated, unable to think of a reply, Allonwë smiled triumphantly, if not full of arrogance.

"HA!" she declared, causing the elder elf to frown. She turned to Natanael and squared her shoulders proudly. "We will be camping here."

"You know we can go just a little way up and make everyone happy," Natanael murmured, glancing anywhere but at the elder.

"We're camping here," Allonwë declared in a lower, more dangerous tone. She was not walking any further tonight.

"You can't!" the elder complained.

"Why? Because it annoys you? Well, you annoy me, so we're even," Allonwë replied.

"This is exactly why I came to live in the woods in the first place!" the elf complained. "Everyone keeps trying to interact with me and take up my breathing space and making noise and being... People! And they expect me to be a people too!" He gestured to himself indignantly.

"Ew," Allonwë commented, wrinkling her nose.

"That's what I said!" the elf agreed. "The nerve! I don't want to share my things, my time, my space, or my mind. It's mine and everyone else can just go away!"

"You know, I never thought I'd find myself agreeing with a guy who could skip rope with his ears, but here I am," Allonwë replied.

Natanael rolled his eyes so hard, he looked out into the woods, eyes landing on a crow that exchanged glances with him before cawing and flying away.

My thoughts exactly, he thought wryly. Not only was Allonwë the most opinionated person he'd ever met. Honestly, the only thing he could see that was alike in the two of them was their dislike of certain people.

While the elder appeared to want the hermit life, Allonwë wanted the unsupervised life. She wanted to do what she felt like whenever she felt like doing it. Sometimes that wasn't a bad thing, but other times it was better that she had supervision, so she didn't accidentally almost burn the entire castle down. A second time.

"You're not going to stay forever, are you?" the elder asked suspiciously.

"Heavens no," Allonwë balked. "I'm just exhausted and ready to have some peace and quiet that doesn't include me standing anymore."

"Oh well, in that case, you should stay the night with me. I don't get many visitors out here," the elf replied.

Natanael did a double take and watched the elf disappear into the brush behind the large stone he'd been sitting on. He stared after him like he'd lost his mind and glanced at Allonwë, who looked just as lost. Hadn't he just stated he didn't want people to come visit him? Allonwë seemed to ask the same silent question, but instantly became distracted by her own curiosity. Where had the old guy gone? He was still talking from the distant muffled sound of his voice, but she couldn't see him through the bramble.

Mustering up the courage, she followed him into the brush and stumbled into a small cave that led to a well-lit area that had apparently been carved into the insides of a very large tree. It was spacious enough to have several rooms and comfortably furnished with soft places to sit that weren't made of sticks and leaves, much to the surprise of the princess. When she exclaimed in surprise, Natanael came crashing in after her, ready to fight off whatever else she'd managed to find that wanted to kill her, only to stop short in the doorway as his eyes adjusted to the light.

"Whoa," he breathed.

"And then," came the voice of the elder elf, who had apparently been in the middle of telling a story as he came back into the main room from a corridor carrying a tray of treats. "I ate some rotten berries and the bears never came back to visit. Strange folk, bears. Though Henrietta was an excellent host when I would go visit her and her cub. They kept lizards as pets." He held up a tray for them and the scent of something bitter sweet reached their noses. "Sap crackers?" he asked, popping one in his mouth. The spine-tingling crunch that emanated from his mouth was like the screech of metal on metal and sent a shiver through the visitors. Graciously, they turned him down, wondering how he had not shattered all of his teeth with the effort.

"We wouldn't want to ruin our supper," Natanael covered for them. Allonwë nodded fervently. He nodded, turning away from them and setting the tray on the table.

"Do you eat meat?" he asked, squinting at them suspiciously.

"What do you consider meat?" Allonwë returned, eyeing him suspiciously.

They stared at each other for the longest before he nodded sagely.

"She asks the right questions," he said, commenting to Natanael. Or at least they hoped that's who he was looking at when he glanced in that direction. If there were some... invisible friends in the house, they probably wouldn't be staying too terribly long after all. He went back into the hallway and Natanael and Allonwë exchanged more than slightly horrified looks.

"What if the meat is people?" Allonwë mouthed. Natanael glanced back at where the elf had disappeared and wished for all that he was worth, that he could put her fears and his own to rest and say that would never happen, but honestly? He couldn't answer that in a way that would alleviate either of them.

"We should be careful, and leave the moment we've got our second wind," Natanael replied softly.

"I agree!" the elf called after them, coming back into the room and dusting his hands off. "You can never be too careful, and the sooner you leave, the better. I don't need you bringing snake men and the apocalypse to my door."

The two travelers stared at him a moment, blinking. "S-sorry, what?"

"Snake men! Undead ones at that," he replied. "People think I'm crazy. But I heard you talking about them. You know what I've seen."

"You've seen the Nagas?" Natanael began cautiously.

"Undead Nagas sent to do the bidding of their evil over-lord and master, Giant Flying Lizards that can eat a man in one gulp but prefer the taste of chai tea and funny stories, Furies that have been magically altered from their natural states into even more terrifying creatures? I've seen it all. And people think I'm the weird one! They live out there in that world where these creatures exist and walk among them wearing glimmer spells like under garments! Plotting who knows what! I do. That's what. I know what they want and that's why I have to live here inside this tree, hidden by magic."

"That would explain why we couldn't see it," Natanael noted. It was strange for this place to be here when it looked like there was nothing but brush and bramble in the surrounding area. With occasional trees here or there. "What do you think they are plotting?"

"I don't think, child; I know!" he replied. "Why, I was there three thousand years ago, at the beginning of the Elf and Dragon Wars. And I remember what it was like to fight on the front line and come back scarred for life - and limb."

"You mean scared?" Natanael asked.

"I know what I meant," he said, rolling up his sleeve to reveal some rather terrifying looking scars on his arms.

Countless.

Some places there were so many that you could only see one rough patch of colorless skin and burn marks patched throughout. A shiver ran down Allonwë's spine.

"They considered me an elder even back then. Brought down a few dragons in my time." The far-off look that crossed his face held nothing but regret and sadness. "Lives are not meant to be taken by others. Doesn't matter what kind of anger or hatred you have for the life you are taking. It's not yours to steal. That's why the undead are rising. They're coming to take back revenge on those that slayed them. And I, for one, will not stand around in the open for them to find me."

Allonwë and Natanael glanced at each other at a loss for words. There really wasn't anything they knew to say or add to the conversation, but now they weren't entirely sure he was insane, so much as paranoid at the world folding in on him. Which, as they had experienced, might not be such a bad thing to be terrified of. Allonwë took a breath and began fidgeting with her fingers.

"These Naga... do you know what they are after?" she asked. "And how to avoid them or... well... stop them from coming after ah... someone?"

"Nagas hate chickens," he replied as a matter-of-factly. "They're related to the basilisk. Distant cousin of sorts. And chickens can kill basilisks. Nagas are stinking terrified of them."

Natanael looked at Allonwë slowly. Her mouth fell open slowly in disbelief. The first laugh of disbelief came from Natanael. And in a moment, both of them were laughing uncontrollably at the ridiculousness of their entire adventure so far.

"It's true! Stop laughing!" the elder elf griped, thinking they were making fun of him.

"No, no - you're right! It is true. We just had no idea when we chucked a chicken in the face of the one that was chasing us," Allonwë replied.

"Chasing you?" the elder elf exclaimed, horrified.

"We lost them," Natanael reassured him. "But it's good to

know that chicken that was hell bent on pecking your face off was good for something."

"Chickens were chasing you too?" the elder elf asked incredulously. "What doesn't chase you?"

"At this point, I'm pretty sure my dignity is the only thing that refuses to keep up with me," Allonwë replied. "That chicken was almost as terrifying as the Naga."

"The chicken didn't try to kill you," Natanael argued flatly.

"The chicken didn't hunt you down and fly at your face, screaming," she retorted.

"Fair enough," Natanael shrugged, not really wanting to get into it.

"Chickens are powerful creatures, boy," the elder elf responded. "Once had one stand between me and an outhouse. The scent of my own fear running down my leg will never leave me."

"Fascinating," Natanael said in a monotone voice.

He did not find it fascinating. In fact, he was more disturbed than anything else. Why, for all that is good in the world, did he get settled with the ones that couldn't have normal conversations? And manners? And sensibility? Common decency even? Or at the very least, common sense. Was it truly too much to ask for a normal situation?

"So, back to my questions about the Nagas," Allonwë continued. "What could they possibly want with... say... a pretty bracelet that could potentially be dangerous? Just... hypothetically speaking?"

"Well, if it's anything like the weapon I fought with in the Great Elf and Dragon Wars, they're probably going to use it to wreak vengeance on the living for the horrible deeds they wrought on the dead," he replied. "They'll start in the east and move their way west. Hitting major cities. Once they've added enough soldiers to their armies, they'll march on those that have caused them the most grief. Either that or they're going to hunt me down like a dog and torture me for all the things I did in the wars. It's why I faked my death. I knew there was no way I could amend for the atrocities I'd done. But perhaps my death would enable them to move past it. I just know there's at least one person out there that swore he'd get his revenge on me, even if it meant finding me beyond the grave. He might be the one behind your undead Naga friends."

"Who's that? And why would he want to hunt you down?" Allonwë asked.

"I... I don't remember names too well. It's been so long," he said, his voice trailing off as that thousand-yard stare came back into his eyes. "I remember his face clearly, though. It'll haunt me for all of my undying days."

"Speaking of names," Allonwë prompted. "What was your name again?"

His glance snapped up to her for a moment, suspicion returning. "I didn't give it."

"I'll tell you mine if you tell me yours," she beamed.

"I didn't give it because I don't remember it," he replied. "And why would I care what your name is?"

"Wait, you forgot your name?" she asked curiously. "Can I name you then?" she said, suddenly much more cheerful.

Natanael closed his eyes and let out a weak groan. This wouldn't end well.

"You're not going to try to keep me as a pet, are you?" the old elf asked suspiciously.

"Nope," Allonwë said. "I'm not allowed to have pets."

He nodded sagely, as if he understood something of immense importance. "Wise, very wise. You can try to tame the wild out of something, but it never truly leaves."

"Who wants to tame the wild out of something? That's the best part!" Allonwë balked.

"I tell you! People are baffling!" the old elf agreed, throwing his hands in the air as if had been a point he'd been trying to make the entire time.

"So, about that name," Allonwë hummed.

Natanael hoped she'd get distracted and forget about that, but she was always one for a personal mission.

"Eh?" the old elf asked, as though he had actually forgotten.

"What about Noland?" Allonwë decided. "You kind of remind me of my great great great great great um great whatever from his paintings in the halls of Sitani castle, and I think the name fits you well."

"Never was one to take another man's name, but I quite like that. Noland," he said as if savoring it on his tongue. "Noooolaaaannd Nolaaaand," he repeated. "Wait... No Land? Are you trying to say I have no land again? I'll have you know this is my tree and my home and no one's gonna take it from me!"

"No, it means noble," Allonwë said. "And I will not take your tree house away from you. I just want to sleep then be on my way."

"Good," Noland nodded, accepting the name. "You can sleep in the spare room. There's only one bed, though. So, you'll have to fight to the death to see who-"

"I call dibs on the floor," Natanael replied quickly.

"Nana! That's not fair!" Allonwë argued. "You won't be able to sleep a wink!"

"Trust me," Natanael replied. "Soldier barracks are not much different. I'll be fine."

"How large is the bed?" Allonwë asked. "I'm sure we can both fit."

"See for yourself," Noland said, leading them to the room he was talking about. There was not much in there save for a tiny bookshelf, a window, and a tiny, tiny bed that one person could probably fit on comfortably, but there was no fitting two people on it. Allonwë deflated for a moment, shoulders sagging, then she perked up almost instantly.

"I have an idea!" she said, skipping to the mattress and pulling it off the bedframe and onto the floor.

"Allonwë what are you doing?" Natanael sighed.

"I'd like to know that myself, lass," Noland agreed.

"We're both going to sleep on the floor!" Allonwë replied cheerfully. "This will be our pillow and we'll lay on it the short way and have our legs hang off the end. That way, we'll both have something soft and hard to lie on and we're even!"

"Makes sense to me," Noland shrugged. "Though I was looking forward to a good fight."

"I'll not fight the pri-ah... lady," Natanael said, catching himself. "I'm sworn to protect her."

"Oh, lighten up, Nana," Allonwë replied. "I've been getting good at my fighting lessons. I'm pretty sure I could give you a run for your money."

"I highly doubt that prin- ah, my lady," Natanael winced at his second screw up in just as many minutes. At this rate, he'd spill her identity all over the countryside and she'd have nothing to do with why they were being chased by bandits this time.

"Fight me!" she said, holding up her fists in a comical gesture. Natanael put one hand on her fist and lowered it. He wasn't even going to humor her on this front. She could get seriously injured, or worse, they'd both lose what little dignity they had left in front of this stranger.

"Why don't I just concede to your bed idea and we call it a night?" Natanael said. At this Allonwë's furrowed brow of determination smoothed into one of pure delight. She smiled so broadly at him it was like looking into the sun itself. By all that was holy, how could she smile like that? It made his heart skip a beat.

"Really?" she all but squeaked. She danced in place for a minute, then turned to Noland. "Can we have a couple of blankets and pillows? Pretty please?"

"Next you're going to demand breakfast," Noland grumbled, heading off to get what they had requested. In moments he was back and handing them some rather dusty looking accouterments. "Here," he said. "Tomorrow I expect you to be out of here! No dawdling!"

"Wouldn't think of it," murmured Natanael as he shut the door behind him as Noland left.

Carefully taking off his armor and laying it to one side, Natanael prepared for sleep with a big yawn. It felt good to shed his armor for once, and while it wasn't the best place to sleep, it was a roof over their head for the night and a somewhat soft place to lay their head.

Laying down on the mattress short ways, he struggled to get comfortable for a moment before he found a sweet spot and relaxed. Across from him, Allonwë was fighting with her pillow to make it just right and pouting when it didn't work the first few times. She finally punched the pillow, a few down feathers floating out of it with the effort, and laid down with a sigh.

"Problem, my lady?" grinned Natanael.

"No," she answered, probably a bit too quickly. "Just trying to get comfortable."

"Doesn't seem to be working," he teased. "You sure you don't want the whole mattress to yourself?"

"Absolutely not!" she shook her head. "I'll not have you sleeping on the floor while I sleep in a nice, soft bed."

"I honestly don't mind, pri-ah-Allonwë," he whispered.

"Well, I do!" she replied in hushed tones as well.

"Why?" he asked.

What could possibly be her reason for caring how well or poor he slept? He was just a bodyguard, and she was a princess. While it was noble of her to share in his predicament, it really made little sense to have them both sleep miserably when at least one of them could be comfortable. Preferably her, as she was more important to the kingdom. He may have been a highly decorated guard, but that still didn't make him any more important than the actual person he was guarding.

"Because you're important to me," she said hesitantly, as if she didn't want to admit that. "And I care what happens to you whether or not you do," she finished indignantly.

Natanael had to close his mouth from saying he was just a lowly guard who didn't deserve that kind of worry because he knew the instant he said it he'd regret it and she would go off on a tangent again.

Still, though, it felt nice to be worried about sometimes. Even though he had done nothing to deserve that worry...

When they finally settled down on the mattress, covered and as comfortable as they were going to get, they laid there facing each other, blinking silently and awkwardly. There was a long, pregnant pause as neither of them knew what to say, do, or how to place their arms.

They completely forgot how to lie normally in a bed whilst laying next to someone else while they were watching. But neither of them wanted to adjust themselves into a better position and admit they were uncomfortable, because doing so would cause the other one to offer them the whole of the mattress, making the excuse to sleep on the floor and neither of them wanted the other to do that. If one of them was going to sleep on the floor, it wasn't going to be the other.

"I'm sleeping on the floor," Natanael said, abruptly pushing himself up.

"You will do no such thing!" Allonwë ordered.

He paused, flushed.

"Settle back down and go to sleep!"

Natanael huffed. "Okay, but I'm facing the wall," he muttered.

"I'm sleeping on the floor," Allonwë declared.

Natanael turned back around and grabbed her arm before she could roll off the mattress.

"Oh, no, you're not!" he countered. "Neither of us is

sleeping on the floor. We're sleeping on this damned mattress if it kills us. This was your idea. We're sticking with it."

"Oh, fine!" Allonwë pouted.

Of course, he would switch tactics like that on her. Using her own plan against her. How rude.

A cackle sounded from deeper inside the house that sent shivers down both of their spines. They had temporarily forgotten they were guests in someone else's home and not in some random inn they were passing by. Allonwë scooted closer to Natanael, her back almost against his.

"What if he murders us in our sleep?" she whispered so quietly Natanael almost missed it. And that was saying something. She rarely spoke that quietly, but when she did, it was usually from a place of genuine fear. She did that when she used to be afraid of thunderstorms. He'd helped her through that fear, too. Now she loved them.

The thing about the storms, however, wasn't just your normal hide under the desk or bed covers and shake in fear. Allonwë had once set the castle on fire in her fear of them, and it had been treacherous waters to navigate that fear and change it into a loving relationship. Well, she hadn't intentionally set the castle on fire to be fair. It had started out with her wandering the halls with an oil lamp to explore one night after everyone had gone to bed. Thunder cracked overhead, making her shriek and jump in fear, dropping the oil lamp and sending it rolling across the floor, spilling oil and fire with it... and knocking over a row of suits of armor. Trying to separate the oil lamp from the fire, she kicked it and the lamp landed in a helmet that went rolling into the kitchens and set the kindling for the stoves on fire.

It had been a mess to handle. She'd cried all night. Natanael was the one that found her hiding in a dumbwaiter and taught her that storms were just clouds that yelled at each other to see which one could spook the other into dissipating first. It had made her laugh and agree to come out so her parents could see she was alright and not turn the castle on its ear looking for her. Ever since, they'd been a pair.

Natanael glanced at the door out of the corner of his eye. On the one hand, he could lie and say everything would be perfectly fine, and there was no chance they were sleeping in the home of an ax murdering elf with ears the length of a longsword. If he didn't placate her fears, they would only get worse and there would be no sleeping for either of them tonight. And they needed their rest to get anywhere tomorrow, let alone face up against untold danger.

Natanael opened his mouth, taking a breath to speak, then paused, closing it again. He didn't want to lie to the princess. That would break their bond of trust, what little there was of that. But he knew she needed calming. He took a breath and let it out slowly.

"No matter what happens, I'll protect you," he said just as softly. He felt her back press against his as she curled into a ball. At first he felt stiff and unsure what to do, but as her breathing evened out and she seemed to have drifted off to sleep, he relaxed a bit, glad she could get some rest.

"Who will protect you?" she asked quietly in the darkness between them.

The thought haunted him more than it should have for the rest of the night.

NEVER TICKLE SLEEPING DRAGONS

Natanael woke first the next morning, the pain in his side from the few cracked ribs he might have pulsating with a deep throb that matched his heartbeat. He suppressed a groan as he rolled over and looked at Allonwë who was still asleep, hair in a mess as she had tossed and turned most of the night on their makeshift half-bed half-floor set up. The sunlight spilled across her torso, slowly making its way up to her face as dawn moved across the sky and shone through the window.

She really was beautiful when she held still long enough Natanael thought. Okay, perhaps that was a bit mean. She was always beautiful, he just didn't get often enough time to appreciate it because he was always trying to keep up with her antics. He was hard on her sometimes, but he was so afraid of losing her that he didn't know exactly how else to act. This journey they were on had only thrown that into more obvious relief as she remained her ever joyful perky self and he buckled down on his no nonsense training.

His thoughts flickered back to the betrothal of her to Elias and his gut twisted that same way again as it had when he heard it the first time.

Stop. He commanded his thoughts not to go in that direction. What good would it do him, anyhow? He was a lowly guard and she was a princess. That kind of thought only ended in disaster on both sides. It wasn't jealousy. It wasn't. He was happy that she'd get to marry her best friend. Even if said best friend didn't love her like that. How horrible it must feel for her to be in a loveless marriage, when Natanael had the freedom to marry for love. Well, maybe not all the freedom.

He wouldn't get to marry *his* best friend even though he could have loved her like that. And it hurt, his betraying thoughts kicked out at him in the fleeting seconds before Allonwë began to stir.

Grateful for the distraction, Natanael gently called her name and touched her shoulder.

"It's time to get up," he murmured. Though he didn't want this moment to end, they needed to keep moving.

"Five more minutes," Allonwë muttered, then seemed to remember where she was. She opened her eyes and looked at Natanael, flushing brightly at their proximity.

Natanael's heart skipped a beat as he blinked back to the present.

"Well," he said at last. "We survived the night."

Allonwë listened for anything. A sound, a nudge, or anything that could give away if the elderly elf was still listening to them.

But there were no sounds, save for the creak of the wood and the gentle breeze blowing through the leaves. It was so eerily quiet, that it set Allonwë on edge, making her cling to Natanael as they got up and looked around for the old man that had let them stay the night.

"What if he was a ghost?" Allonwë whispered. "He just

disappeared without a trace, and this whole place is covered in dust! I didn't notice this much dust last night…"

"He's probably out hunting for berries or whatever that weird old man does in his spare time," Natanael tried to reassure her, but the quietness of the house set him on edge as well. There was just something off about it. Like the air was displaced and things were watching them from the corners of every shadow.

"Let's just leave a thank you note and leave," Allonwë suggested.

For once, Natanael agreed with her. There was no time to lose in getting back on their way, strange ghost elf or not. They didn't have time to wait around and see if he came back. Instructing Allonwë to write the letter while he returned the mattress to its rightful place on the frame, Natanael looked around for anything they could have missed. When he was certain they had everything, they made their way to the door and found it locked in very intricate ways.

Ways that could only be locked from the inside.

Another shiver ran down Allonwë's spine as Natanael carefully undid all the intricate locks and things on the door and quickly ushered the princess out. They made their way down the slope of the hill the tree rested upon, and took up their heading again. When they had traveled for hours, Allonwë was crying with the effort to convince him to take a break.

"This is it," she said. "This is how we die. Not taken out by horrifying creatures that can't die. Not saving the damsel in distress and heroically giving our lives for the townsfolk. But of starving belly and thirst and aching feet and bones!"

"We've only been walking for five hours, pr-Allonwë," Natanael said flatly. "You'll live."

"Have some compassion, man! I ran out of water three hours ago," Allonwë bemoaned.

"I told you not to gulp it," Natanael replied. "And to stop talking so much to make yourself thirsty."

"Nana!" Allonwë stood up and put her hands on her hips. "How dare you accuse me of talking too much! I talk a perfectly normal amount thank you very much and I'll have you know-"

"Allonwë," Natanael said flatly, turning to glare at her in the face. Allonwë's words caught in her throat, heat creeping into her face as if she'd been caught doing just what she declared she wasn't doing. Which, of course, she was, but Natanael had also been much closer than she'd expected and when they nearly came nose to nose, her mind had scrambled and there was a huge blank space in her thoughts.

How had he done that?

Natanael continued, bringing Allonwë's soul back from another plane of existence where it had screamed into the void.

"We'll get you some water. We'll get to a resting place soon. The more ground we put between us and those things, the safer we'll be until we can continue searching tomorrow with more provisions." He spoke levelly and calmly, as if to a startled child, but the look on his face was of tempered patience. "There's a stream up ahead. I'll go get water momentarily. But first, we need to follow along the path and find a place for shelter. Understand?"

Allonwë gave a small nod, her shoulders pressing against her ears as she'd shrunk back, realizing she'd gone a bit too far with the dramatics. Either that, or something was bothering Natanael, and he wasn't able to focus on his normal patience with Allonwë's shenanigans.

"Good," Natanael stated firmly. He turned and released the princess from his stare and took a slow breath as he put a hand across his midsection casually.

Allonwë blinked. Natanael was hurt. Fear spiked through the princess's chest and settled cold in her stomach like frozen marbles. If Natanael was trying to hide his pain, that potentially meant he was much more badly hurt than he was willing to let Allonwë know, lest the princess panic. But despite wanting to do just that, Allonwë steadied her nerves by taking a few long, slow, breaths in through her nose and let them out through her mouth. There was a lengthy silence as they continued forward, Allonwë trying to find a way to bring it up.

"I... know how to sew if you have any open wounds," she said slowly.

Natanael stiffened for a brief second, then pointed ahead of them. Almost like he'd seen something just in the nick of time saving him from answering, or like he was glad for a subject change.

"There's a cave up there," he said, striding towards it briskly. "Wait here, I'll check it out."

"I'll do no such thing!" Allonwë balked, running up behind him. She lowered her voice to a harsh whisper. "If you're injured, you'll not stand a chance if there's a team of pirating brigadier goblins or something in there!"

"I don't have time to point out everything wrong with that sentence, so I'm just going to ignore it," Natanael replied. "Stay here and make sure nothing sneaks up behind me."

"Nonsense, Nana!" Allonwë declared. "Obviously I'm going in first!" And without hesitation, the princess marched past him before Natanael could stop her and entered the cave. With a long-suffering sigh, Natanael walked as fast as he could towards the cave entrance, wishing he had the stamina to run without severe stabbing pain in his side.

"Allonwë!" he whispered hoarsely. "Come back here this instant!" Despite the quiet tone, his voice echoed loudly, and he quickly realized this was a much deeper cave than it appeared to be. It wasn't just deep and dark, it was cavernous. And there were only two explanations for cavernous caves. They'd been dug by one of two creatures: dwarves - which were abrasive towards elves (Allonwë would probably love them) - and, well, dragons. Sworn enemies of elves.

When he heard Allonwë gasp in awe and coo at the sight of something pretty, his heart sank into his boots. Dwarves and dragons alike loved treasure. That's why they got along so well. The two made excellent scavenger teams. Especially when gold could be gained from a pirating standpoint. It was hard to say no to a dwarf riding a dragon. Especially when the dragon threatened to breathe fire - or other noxious fumes - into your face if you didn't agree to hand over everything shiny. Natanael quickly made his way into the cave, following the sound of Allonwë's voice as she found more and more treasure.

"Please be a dwarf hoard, please be a dwarf hoard, please be a dwarf hoard," Natanael chanted under his breath as he came to the main part of the cave.

There were mounds of gold, suits of armor from various races lining the walls with crowns and pearls and glittering weapon sheaths handing off of them. There were goblets and chests and gold coins and silver platters and all manner of beautiful things around them and Allonwë had found a gold trimmed mirror to admire her reflection in as she tried on some earrings.

"Allonwë!" he hissed.

"These look darling!" Allonwë said, turning towards Natanael. "What do you think?"

"I think we've stumbled across either a dwarf or a dragon hoard, or worse, both!" he said. "And they don't take kindly to people stealing their things."

"Oh," Allonwë said, looking around. "That makes much more sense than my theory of a magical cave goblin." She gave a small gasp. "Nana! Can we wait for the dwarf to come back? Maybe they can teach me how to be gross in front of my parents! That'll keep me from having other do court responsibilities for years yet! They'd absolutely abhor it! Maybe I can even learn some new swear words - oh, think of the possibilities!" she giggled, clapping her hands.

"It might not be a dwarf hoard, and our lives could be at stake here," Natanael warned.

"Oh, don't be over dramatic Nana!" Allonwë tsked.

She leaned her hand against the wall casually, trying to exude confidence as she place her other hand on her hip and cast a grin at Natanael. The wall rumbled beneath her hand and Allonwë paused.

"Was that an earthquake?" she asked.

But Natanael wasn't looking at her.

Natanael's eyes were trailing upward - far upwards, as his lips parted in fearful awe and his brows knitted together in silent confirmation that his worst fear was indeed true. Allonwë followed his gaze upward, looking at the ceiling that was now looking back with large, glowing gold eyes, framed in a large scaley face with nostrils that flared as the scales glittered bright purple blending into a darker hue through the spikes and horns on its face. The underbelly was that of near pearlescent. Allonwë slowly removed her hand from what she thought had been a wall, but was actually the dragon's belly. The eyes squeezed shut, and it made the sound of rumbling earth again.

Three rumbles just like before... almost like...

A chuckle?

"Allonwë get behind me," Natanael said quickly.

Allonwë didn't argue, suddenly unable to think of balking at the idea. Who knew dragons were so ridiculously gigantic? Certainly not her. No wonder they were so difficult to fight against! Natanael's hand went to his sword, but Allonwë had just enough mind to stop him.

"Wait," she said. "It hasn't attacked us. Maybe it's friendly."

"Allonwë," Natanael warned. "It's a dragon."

"A pretty dragon," Allonwë agreed, admiring the scales.

She cleared her throat. "Hello! Please don't eat us! We're just passing through and we're looking for shelter and food! You wouldn't have anything to spare, would you?"

Heavens above, she sounded like those horrible travelers that started all this mess.

"I don't like strangers wandering into my den," the dragon said firmly.

"Oh," Allonwë said, feeling slightly less brave at that statement. "Well, I'm Allonwë, and this is my bo- uh- friend, Natanael. You can call him Nana. Everyone does."

Natanael did a double take at Allonwë, then looked back at the dragon.

"Now if you tell us your name, we'll not be strangers!" Allonwë continued.

"True…" the dragon replied slowly. Another rumble.

"Goodness, that's quite the sneeze you have there!" Allonwë said.

"That was my name," the dragon replied.

"Oh," Allonwë said, realizing they probably didn't have an elvish equivalent to sneezing-earthquake. "OH! I can give you a name we can pronounce! It can be a strong, amazing nickname!"

"Allonwë don't-" warned Natanael, but to no avail.

"I'll call you Charlie!" Allonwë said triumphantly, ignoring her bodyguard.

"Allonwë you can't name a Great Dragon Charlie," he hissed.

"You're right, that's not nearly dignified enough," Allonwë hummed in thought.

"That's not what I-" Natanael began.

"I've got it!" Allonwë cut him off. "Charles Harold Alexander Raoul Luxemburg Ignatius the Excellent!"

Natanael closed his eyes, resisting the urge to cover his face with his hands and reconsider his life choices. He knew exactly what each first letter of that ridiculously long name spelled and he wanted to smack the princess in the back of the head for it. They were about to be skewered by a dragon for calling it ridiculous names. On the list of possible ways he could get killed, this hadn't quite made the list, but it wasn't too far off from the other ridiculous things he imagined would kill him until now. Most of them involved lots and lots of fire. This way probably wouldn't end up any differently actually, come to think of it.

"That sounds like a strong name," the dragon said happily.

Natanael looked stunned.

"That... it is," he said hesitantly, looking at Allonwë, who shrugged at him.

"My friend would like that name," the dragon said. "But..."

"But what?" Allonwë asked, enraptured over the talking dragon as Natanael was more concerned with being ambushed by other dragons.

"I lost him," the dragon said softly. "I've been searching for days and I can't find him. When I get stressed, I collect things, but he gets mad at me when I steal from castles. He says it's too dangerous, but I can't help it. These things are just so shiny!"

"I completely agree!" Allonwë nodded. "Shiny things always make me feel better. Like this one time, I was playing hide and go scare with Nana, and I hid behind this tapestry waiting to jump out and see if I could scare him, right? Only, the wall opened up behind me!"

The dragon gasped softly.

"Yes! I was so shocked when I tumbled backwards into a room full of strange old artifacts I didn't know what to do!" Allonwë continued. "Until I looked around and saw this really nice shiny bracelet that went amazingly with my eyes - do you know how hard it is to come by things that go great with eyes like mine?"

"But they look amazing!" the dragon replied, equally enraptured by Allonwë.

"That is the sweetest thing anyone has ever said to me!" Allonwë nearly cried, putting a hand to her chest. "See Nana! I finally found someone to appreciate me for who I am. He likes my eyes and he likes shiny things! This dragon is my soul friend!"

Natanael tried not to let out another long-suffering sigh. "At any rate, we need to find that shiny bracelet of yours. It's still missing," he said flatly.

"Missing?" the dragon gasped.

"Yes! It was stolen from me!" Allonwë said dramatically.

"No!" the dragon gasped again.

"No," Natanael replied. "You lost a bet with three random travelers that wanted to kidnap you and kill me."

"No way!" the dragon gasped even more dramatically.

"Yes! And they're undead!" Allonwë said with a flourish.

The dragon was scandalized.

Gods, they were a perfect match for each other, Natanael groaned.

Then Allonwë gasped. "But oh no! Your friend! Where did he go?"

The dragon sobered from his shock and hung his head a bit. "He went out hunting and I got distracted and went away from our meeting spot and then I couldn't find my way back and I panicked and made a den."

"It's a lovely den," Allonwë soothed, putting a hand on Charlie's nose. "It would have cheered me up too."

"Thank you," Charlie replied.

"Oh! I have it!" Allonwë declared. "We'll help you look for your friend!"

"Really?" Charlie perked up.

"Allonwë we can't," Natanael reminded her. "We have our own quest."

"Oh... right," Allonwë deflated.

"I can help you with your quest! I'm good at finding shiny things. Especially if they have a certain smell!" Charlie replied.

"Oh! Nana!" Allonwë said, turning around. "Your sword! You stabbed the thing and then it came back to life! Your sword might still smell like it!"

"The bracelet is alive?" Charlie asked.

"No, the travelers that attacked us," Allonwë explained.

"Ohhh," Charlie nodded. "That makes more sense."

"I wouldn't wish that smell on anyone," Natanael replied, getting them back on the subject. "But if he's willing, and it helps us get done with this quest as soon as possible, I'm willing to try."

"Perfect!" Allonwë beamed. "We can help you find your friend, then you can help us find the bracelet!" she clapped with glee.

"I like that idea," Charlie said. "That's so brave of you to help me."

"Nana is the best tracker I've ever seen," Allonwë smiled warmly. "If anyone can find your friend, it's him."

"That's amazing!" Charlie said in awe.

"First things first," Natanael said. "What does your friend look like, and would we be able to see them from the sky if you flew up high enough?"

Charlie considered his questions. "He is pretty small. Kind of your size or smaller. It would be hard to see them from the air."

"OH!" Allonwë gasped at the idea of a tiny baby dragon. "What is his name? I know a spell that can make my voice really loud and shout his names from high until we get his attention! I once used it to annoy my parents for three days. Well, the three days was an accident. I meant to only use it for three hours, but I figured out what I did wrong and it should work properly this time."

"Do I need to remind you we're trying to hide from people chasing us?" Natanael argued.

Though he remembered that incident well. Family dinner wasn't the same for three days, with her screaming halfway across the castle to pass the salt. She'd originally done it to make herself easier for a partially deaf member of the staff to hear her better, which left said member giggling the whole time. Her parents found it less amusing, but they also didn't know the real reason behind why she did it, either.

"Do I need to remind you, Nana, that we now have a dragon on our side?" Allonwë countered.

"Fair point," Natanael conceded. "Continue."

Surely, even the undead couldn't stand up against a dragon, he reasoned. Maybe this was finally turning in their favor.

"This spell will make me capable of being heard for miles! If you carry us up high enough, I can shout for him to find us and tell them to meet us over here! What do you think?" Allonwë asked.

"That's perfect!" Charlie said, getting excited. "His name is Old Elf. Or at least that's what I call him."

They planned out what to say and how to direct him to the cave and when they were certain they had it down; they headed outside, but Natanael hesitated. Were they really going to do this? Fly in the sky on the back of a dragon? This was also not on his list of ways he expected to die with Allonwë dragging him along, but it definitely wasn't the weirdest thing that had happened to them so far.

Taking a deep breath, he helped Allonwë onto Charlie's back, joining her shortly after with some difficulty. When Charlie launched into the air, Allonwë screamed with delight, but Natanael screamed in pure fear, before clamping his mouth shut and grabbing onto his charge with a grip that nearly knocked the air out of her. When they leveled out and Charlie's wings caught the currents, steadying the ride, Natanael's grip lessened and Allonwë let out a giggle.

"Are you going to be okay, Natanael?" she asked, just barely loud enough for the other elf to hear over the wind.

"I'm getting there," Natanael said. "Let's just get this over with."

Allonwë set the spell to make her voice louder, and they spent the better part of an hour shouting from the skies down into the trees below, and it was all Allonwë could do before she started going hoarse. When at last they landed back at the cave, they looked around for any sign of Charlie's friend, but there was nothing.

"Maybe he's on his way," Allonwë reassured him, her voice slightly squeaky.

There was a crunching sound as someone stumbled through the leaves and caught their attention. Natanael went in defense mode, standing before Allonwë cautiously, but when a frail, old - ancient by the familiar, ridiculously long ears - gaunt looking blonde elf stumbled out of the woods and dusted himself off, they hesitated. He looked around, seemingly bewildered, and caught sight of Charlie.

He made an odd grumbling noise, then added, "There you are, girl!" Noland warbled. "I've been worried sick!"

"Old Elf!" Charlie cried, half running, half flapping his way over to Noland. "I was so worried about you!"

"I'm fine, girl, don't worry about me," he quieted the crying dragon. "You all worry too much about me when you should be more worried about those strange birds that have been flying about. Have you noticed them? I think they're spies of some sort."

"But it's my job to worry over you!" Charlie scolded. "What if you don't eat properly or something happened to you? I'd never forgive myself!"

"Bah!" he waved. "I can take care of myself," he reassured the scaley beast. "What do you two want now?" he asked, directing his attention to the elves before him.

"They helped me find you, so now I'm gonna help them find their missing bracelet!"

"Missing bracelet?" Noland barked. "You haven't been hoarding again, have you?"

Charlie looked as sheepish as a dragon could. "Well, yes, but that's not-"

"What have I told you about hunting treasure? It's dangerous!" Noland scolded.

"I know," Charlie sighed. "But I panicked when I couldn't find you and they helped me find you, so now I'm going to help them!"

"What kind of bracelet is it? And why is it so special?" Noland asked.

"Well, remember that bracelet we mentioned before? It's actually really pretty and really dangerous, but some undead guys took it and now they're trying to kidnap me and we're trying to prevent that from happening and stop the bracelet from being used now that it's in the wrong hands," Allonwë summarized. "We think it's a weapon of mass destruction, like the one you mentioned you used in the elf and dragon wars."

There was a long silence bordering on awkward. Allonwë and Natanael exchanged looks before glancing back at Noland, who took a breath through his nose slowly.

"No," he said firmly, pointing a finger at the dragon.

"But Old Elf!" the dragon complained.

"Now's not the time," Noland argued.

"Then I'll make it the time!" Charlie argued. "I'm not letting someone who went out of their way to help me leave without repaying them. I owe them."

The two of them exchanged a meaningful glance. One that seemed to carry a long, silent conversation only they could understand. At last, Noland looked away with a sigh and a groan.

"Fine, but I'm coming with you," Noland conceded. "But first you're not going anywhere without some lunch."

"That may not be such a good idea if you are as old as I think you are," Natanael said. He also didn't want this weird old man to travel with them.

"You were just saying you wanted help. Have you changed your minds so easily?" the old elf asked.

"I don't want to put your lives in danger," Natanael said. "But... we are desperate for any help we can get. That bracelet was a powerful weapon. We don't know what things that can be done with it, but if it's as great as the stories surrounding it say it is, then I'm worried whomever has it now will endanger the lives of everyone. I will not sugarcoat what we are dealing with here. This is dangerous. Very dangerous. But that's why we need help. We cannot do this alone anymore."

"The creatures that came after us looked human, but when Natanael slew one, it melted into a puddle, then retook its original form. Normal means can't kill it," Allonwë added. "They're after me too. I don't know why. I don't understand what I have to do with all of this, but I'm terrified of what they'll do to me when they find me."

"Come in and sit down for lunch. I think I can explain a few things," Noland said.

Shaking his head, and led them all back to the hidden tree house where a steady stream of smoke was rising from the small chimney poking out of the top of the leaves. There was a table out back and some chairs and a space next to the table for Charlie to sit.

Allonwë was seated awkwardly on a stump, Natanael choosing to stand behind her, Noland brought out a large pot of soup for all to enjoy as well as some fresh bread, cheese, and freshly picked cucumbers, bell peppers, and tomatoes from a garden just past the house and in a small clearing in the woods where it could get sunshine. He brought out a pot of herbal tea for everyone to drink and finally sat down at the head of the table himself.

"Wow, this is so much food!" Allonwë commented. "It

smells amazing!" For once, her fear of becoming the food for the table seemed to ebb away.

"Of course, it does," Charlie grinned. If dragons could grin, that's certainly what it was doing now. "The Old Elf is the best cook for miles besides me."

"Yeah, if you like regurgitated meat," Noland laughed.

Allonwë hesitated in taking a bite of her food. "Regurgitated meat?" There was horror no her face that asked 'Did you chew this meat before you put it in the stew?' but she didn't have the guts to ask it out loud.

"He's talking about the ONE TIME we met and made friends and he fed me a fish and I ate part of it and gave him the other half, but it had already been in my mouth so it was covered in spit," Charlie replied.

"Oh, thank the Gods," Allonwë sighed with relief.

"What? It's good like that!" Charlie commented, deep and guttural. She laid beside the table as Noland threw some bread and whole bell peppers at her mouth and she caught them midair, chewing thoughtfully. "Old Elf is the best."

"I'm not as deserving of those compliments you give me," Noland added, handing Charlie some cucumbers too.

"What do you mean?" Charlie asked, wide eyed. "You're the nicest person I've ever met!"

"Maybe the weirdest person I've ever met," Allonwë muttered under her breath where only Natanael could hear. He nudged her back casually, as if to tell her to stop.

"If you knew me in my previous life before I came to live in the woods, you would understand how much blood I have on my hands. You would think differently of me," he said, letting out a long sigh as the table fell silent.

"What do you mean? Old Elf, you're scaring me," Charlie said softly.

"I once had a name," he continued.

"You said you didn't remember it," Charlie said. "That's why I call you Old Elf."

"I know, child," he said with a small but grim smile. "I was once an elf of great power. An important one too. I went up against a man of despicable power and lost all my former glory. I became the withered husk of an elf you see today. Before all of that, they knew me as Noland, Prince of Sitani Castle, and heir to the throne of Kutawë."

There was a gasp from Allonwë, who stood up abruptly. "You're my... There's no way-" she began, then remembered the portrait in the strange room she'd found the bracelet in. The painting of him struck a remarkable resemblance and was one reason she'd nicknamed him Noland in the first place. "You're my great, great, great, great, great, great, great, great, great-"

"Not that great. I'm old, but I'm not that old. Well, maybe I am-" Noland doubted himself for a moment. "Wait, does that make you-" but he was interrupted with a break of laughter.

"There's no way!" Charlie declared. "You could never be a monster like him!" she said. "He was huge! He killed tons of dragons with that weapon of... his..." Suddenly Charlie's laughter died off as his eyes went to Allonwë's. Their gaze met across the table, the fear in Allonwë's eyes bringing Charlie's fear to the surface. The bracelet Allonwë had lost. The weapon of mass destruction... it had been Noland's weapon. This Noland. "But... Sir Noland... was the one that... killed my parents... my family..."

There was silence from Noland as he bowed his head and couldn't seem to look up from the table.

"The bracelet," Allonwë said. "You knew what we meant when we were talking about it in the clearing... How dangerous it could be... because you've seen its power in action... haven't you?"

"I have," Noland replied.

"But I thought you said you didn't remember anything of

your past," Charlie interjected. She still didn't seem to accept any of this was true.

"It wasn't until this young lady here gave me a name that I remembered it as my own, and the burden of sins that came with it," Noland said.

"Were you caught up in the wars?" Allonwë asked softly.

"Partly," Noland said. "I had been misled into believing the dragons were the reason behind a great deal of evil things happening in the kingdom. It was of a magic that we elves couldn't use. A magic that is rare and ancient. A type that can only be used by certain creatures."

"Necromancy..." Allonwë whispered. At this, Noland looked up, surprised that she knew.

"By the time I had uncovered the truth, three wars had come and gone and I had more blood on my hands than I could ever atone for. I went after the beast that had caused all this bloodshed and fought him with everything I had. I thought I killed him that day. Thought I put an end to all this."

"But...?" Natanael could sense there was something more.

"But if what you say is true, then he survived, and he is going to use the weapon to resurrect every dragon and elf killed in those wars to take over every other race in the world. And if he succeeds, there will be no stopping him," Noland finished.

Lesson 8

SOME SHINY OBJECTS WERE YOUR FRIENDS

Charlie stood abruptly, nearly knocking the table off balance as she did so. She got a running start to launch herself into the air and took off. Noland called after her, trying to get her to come back, but to no avail.

"Maybe she just needs time to cool off," Allonwë said.

"You don't understand," Noland said with a sigh. "She's... directionally challenged. If she goes off without a heading, she'll get lost."

"Oh no," Allonwë said. "Wait! Natanael is an excellent tracker! Nana, you can find her again, right? Oh, please say you can find her..."

Natanael sighed, rubbing his face. "We'll have to hurry. It looks like she went northeast back towards the cave she built. Let's hope she remembers how to get there from here, so we're not searching all over the place." He spoke slowly, as if measuring his words. Both Allonwë and Noland looked at him strangely.

"Something's wrong with you," Noland stated bluntly. "What is it?"

"It's nothing," Natanael said, shaking his head. "We need

to get moving if we're going to find her before we need to leave."

Allonwë noticed the sweat forming on Natanael's brow and frowned.

"Son, you look ill," Noland continued to press.

"Do you want to find your dragon or not?" Natanael snapped.

"If she's headed towards the cave, then we know where to find her," Noland shook his head.

"Nana? What's he talking about? What's wrong?" Allonwë asked. Then she remembered how he winced the other day, snapping her like he had just now. "You've been like this since the attack with the Nagas. You were hurt, weren't you?"

"I'm fine," Natanael replied firmly.

Nolan came up to him and jabbed him in the ribcage with a finger, and Natanael nearly doubled over with a heavy groan. He took a breath through his nose and let it out through his mouth several times before he carefully straightened whilst glaring at Noland and holding his side.

"Rib's broken," Noland declared. "Can't fight undead with broken bones."

"Nana!" Allonwë exclaimed, moving to his side and reaching out for him.

He held up a hand to stop her and she held back, not wanting to hurt him further. She opened and closed her fists, not sure what to do or how to hold herself. Natanael had never been this badly hurt in her shenanigans, and those creatures had been after her. This was her fault.

"I can handle this," Natanael said.

"You should have said something sooner," Noland scolded him. "Dragons have healing magic."

"How was I supposed to know?" Natanael said.

"Don't know unless you ask, so stop trying to be stoic and start trying to be smart," Noland said. "Let's find-" he made some grumbling noises that equated to Charlie's dragon name, "and see if we can't get you healed."

"I've got to learn how to say that," Allonwë commented under her breath to distract herself as she followed Natanael as they started their heading in the direction that Charlie went. If she didn't think too hard about Natanael's condition, maybe a solution would pop into her head. She was good at spontaneous solutions.

They walked for the better part of an hour until they reached the cave, Natanael's movements getting slower and slower as he exerted himself more. When they went inside, they found Charlie with a new trinket in the glittering, golden cave. It was something from one chest in the corner. The wooden frame opened to reveal a half empty chest of glittering gold and jewels.

Noland called out to Charlie who stood, turned her back on him, and laid down in the piles of treasure, causing a great ruckus of falling coins and suits of armor toppling over and a great clatter of scales against the precious metals as she did so.

"I know you are angry with me," Noland began. "And I owe you so much."

"How dare you speak to me!" Charlie bellowed. "You owe me my family!"

"That I do," Noland nodded. "And no amount of apologizing that I can do will bring them back."

"I always swore that I would find their soul stones one day. That I would take them back so they could be reborn," Charlie said, her voice heavy with emotion as she spoke.

"What's a soul stone?" Allonwë asked.

"It's... the last drop of blood that falls from a dragon when it's killed," Noland explained sadly. "It hardens into a stone and becomes an extremely powerful magical item. I crafted a weapon that would take the form of a gauntlet or bracelet in times of peace, but that would transform into a sword in moments of danger." He looked at Allonwë, who was having a flashback to the books she'd read in the library regarding the old bracelet she'd found.

"So, like a Heart Stone?" she asked.

"Aye, that's what the Mages of Barlow called it," Noland nodded, surprised again by her knowledge. "As it would pulse with the heartbeat of the dragon, it belonged to."

"Soul stones are sacred!" Charlie snarled. "They're the life force. The soul of the dragon formed into a stone that can be reborn again!"

"They can be reborn from them?" Noland asked, shocked.

"Yes! Why do you think they're so important to us?" Charlie demanded. "Important to me! I could have seen my family again, but you stole them from me!"

"That stone... I made the stone of the white dragon into the bracelet. If what your friends here say is true, I think that's the same bracelet that has fallen into the hands of whomever is trying to kill them," Noland said urgently.

"What... what are you saying?" Charlie asked, looking over her shoulder, not fully understanding the urgency in his tone. "My sister's stone was turned into a bracelet?"

"A weapon of mass destruction. The weapon they are looking for now. The one they are trying to find- don't you understand?" Noland said. "Your sister's stone is still alive! You can find it and help save her and she may be reborn again!"

Charlie's eyes lit up, and she stood, turning in place, coins and treasure falling out of her scales as she stomped the ground beneath her feet. She shook the cave, knocking some of the dirt down from the ceiling as she did so, and got down into Noland's face, breathing hot air onto him that was tinged with the heat of fire.

"Where's. My. Sister?" she demanded.

"That's what we're trying to figure out," Natanael said, bringing Charlie's attention over to him. He stepped forward and wobbled on his feet. "We need... to find them... before it's too... late..." Natanael collapsed to his knees, and Allonwë scrambled to catch him before he fell to the ground.

She eased him to the cave floor, calling out his name. She felt his forehead. He was running a fever. She looked up at Charlie. "Can you heal him? Please! I can't lose him!"

Charlie looked surprised. "I-I can try." She moved her nose over to him and told Allonwë to step back.

If Natanael died here, there was no way she could continue this mission. And if there was no way she could finish the mission, there was no telling what was going to happen to that bracelet. If someone was doing necromancy and they wanted that stone, what could it mean for the country of Kutawë? Nothing good, that was for sure. Everything hinged on him and making sure he lived through this. Not to mention it would destroy her world if she lost the one person she could trust beyond anyone else. Her best friend and confidant.

Charlie put her nose to his chest and Natanael grunted in pain as the dragon's eyes slipped closed, focusing. There was a glowing light between them, and for a moment, Allonwë's heart stopped as she thought Charlie was breathing fire onto him, but the light wasn't warm. It was cold. There was a sickening *snap!* and Natanael cried out in pain, curling in on himself. Charlie pulled away and huffed through her nose, smoke tendrils forming out of her nostrils.

"He's going to need to sleep that off," she said. "He's going to be really sore when he wakes up. But it's no longer poking into his organs. It should heal completely in a few hours."

"We need to get him back to the tree house," Noland said.

"You can stay in my cave," Charlie suggested. "It might be better not to move him too much if we can help it."

"Do you have anything soft we can put him on?" Allonwë asked.

"Just gold, which I think is soft," Charlie replied.

"It'll have to do," Noland said. "Come on, girl, help me get him up."

It was a rough night as they all slept in the cave, Allonwë could hardly sleep for fear Natanael would need something or that he wouldn't recover properly. She was scared. Really, truly scared that she might lose him in this mess.

It wasn't until the wee hours of the morning that she finally fell asleep and was startled awake not three hours later by Natanael lurching upwards with a gasp as if he'd just had the worst nightmare of his life. Allonwë scrambled to get up and check on him, heart hammering in her chest.

"We can't stay here-" Natanael was saying. "What time is it? How many days have we lost?"

"Relax, relax," Allonwë said, calming him down. "It's only been a night. Charlie healed your ribs. You needed to sleep off the fever."

"We can't lose much more time, Allonwë," Natanael said. "We're going to be caught by those Naga and lose the bracelet if we don't hurry."

"The girl is right," Noland said from the mouth of the cave as he came back inside. He'd been out to the tree house apparently, as he'd come back with a sack full of supplies and gear ready to embark on a quest to find the bracelet with them. "You can relax. There's a reason the undead snake people are searching for you."

Natanael and Allonwë exchanged looks of curiosity.

"So, you know why they want to kidnap me and kill Natanael?" Allonwë asked.

"Because I put a clause in the spell on the bracelet that it would only work with our bloodline. It also won't let go of the wearer unless strictly told to let them go," Noland said. "I didn't want it slipping off my wrist when I wasn't paying attention or falling into the wrong hands, much like it has now, and be usable by just anyone! Now they need you to activate it so that they can unleash armies of the undead upon the world."

"Wait, '*our* bloodline'?" Natanael repeated, not having remembered telling him that Allonwë was the Princess of Kutawë. He looked between them, wondering if she had blabbed to Noland while Natanael had been out cold.

"I'm not stupid, boy. I can put two and two together," Noland replied. "When she said you're my great, great-"

"Great, great, great, great-" Allonwë nodded, continuing with him.

"Great, great whatever; I realized that's why the snake people were after you. It all started to come together. Smart thinking with that chicken. We're gonna need someone like you on this journey. Your boy here is a little slow. We need quick thinkers to fight the undead," Noland declared to Allonwë.

"Don't tell anyone about that. We have enough trouble as it is," Natanael warned.

"I said I'm old, not stupid," Noland replied. "Catch up."

"Old Elf," Charlie said, catching his attention. "I don't want you to come," she added darkly.

"I'm afraid I have to," Noland replied.

"Why?" Charlie asked.

"Because I have to atone for some of the evil I brought into this world," Noland said. "I don't expect forgiveness, but I do expect atonement if from no one else, then from myself."

"I won't forgive you, even if we get my sister back," Charlie said.

"I know that," Noland said softly. "But know that you were the sunlight in my life for the time you allowed me to know you. Thank you."

Charlie snorted derisively, but said nothing more.

"Let's get moving," Natanael said. "There's no telling how long it'll take those Naga to catch up with us."

"Do you even know where you're going?" Noland said.

"W-Well," Natanael began slowly, hesitating for the first time on directions since they started the journey. Allonwë noted this and was surprised. Her eyes became the size of dinner plates when his shoulders slumped slightly and he admitted, "No. I don't."

"Then you need me," Noland said. "I know where to at least begin looking for the bracelet."

"Where's that?" Natanael asked.

"In the old war grounds," Noland answered.

"That's all the way at the southern border!" Natanael exclaimed. "It'll take us weeks!"

"Not if Charles Harold Alexander Raoul Luxembourg Ignatius the Excellent lets us fly on her back," Allonwë said triumphantly.

"Who are all those people?" Noland asked, confused.

"You can call me Charlie. It's fine," the dragon replied.

"I thought your name was-" Noland made the growling noise again.

"Well, I enjoy going by Charlie now," the dragon complained.

"That's fine, lass, I was just confused," Noland said, holding up a hand to show he meant no disrespect.

"And the answer is no, you can't fly on me," Charlie said firmly.

"But we flew on you earlier," Allonwë said. "Why the change of heart?"

"Because *he's* coming," Charlie said, nodding at the old elf. "I'm not letting the man who killed my siblings ride on my back."

"Child," the Old Elf said, stepping forward. "I know I have no right to request this from you, but I'm afraid I must. What if I offered you a deal?"

"I don't make deals with murderers," Charlie said firmly.

"Just hear me out," Noland pleaded, babbling. "If you ferry me safely to our destination, I will do everything in my power to return your sister's soul stone to you. I will destroy the weapon and make it so that no one can ever create such a thing again."

There was a beat as Charlie let that information sink in. Natanael wondered if she was going to roast him where he stood, but Charlie lowered her head and looked at him sadly.

"You really think we can save her?" Charlie asked softly.

"If we work together, yes," Noland said.

Another heavy pause as Natanael held his breath.

"I will do it," Charlie said at last. "I will carry you in safety... You may ride on my back."

"Thank you," Noland said softly.

"Don't thank me," Charlie growled. "I'm doing this for my sister. Not for you."

"I know that too," Noland replied.

"Good. Now let's go," Charlie declared, turning and laying down to allow them to climb onto her back. They clambered up her scales, which were surprisingly smooth to the touch, and settled on her back. Natanael took a few deep breaths to steel himself for the launch again. He screamed again as Charlie shot into the air and held on for dear life.

"We should have made a harness and saddle!" he yelled through gritted teeth.

Allonwë screeched with delight, that turned into laughter as they leveled out. "Where would the fun be in that?" she asked over the bluster of wind and the sounds of Charlie's wing flaps.

They held onto each other as Noland gave Charlie directions, the flight over the fields dangerously far below them where the cattle looked like tiny ants compared to how large they normally looked up close and personal.

Natanael tried to hold on to Allonwë and force her to remain in one spot rather than craning her neck around to look at everything they passed, but the princess wouldn't have any of it. She fussed at him and continued to look around as if this wasn't the most terrifying thing they'd done yet.

Sure, they'd ridden the dragon once before, but only for about the better part of an hour. This was going to take much longer than that and gave them a greater chance of being seen and attacked from below by Elven soldiers. But Charlie stuck to the cloud cover and when there weren't clouds to hide in, she soared higher so there was little to no shadow to be seen below. And if there was a shadow, it'd look more like a bird flying than a dragon carrying three passengers.

The weeks that it would have taken them to travel from the eastern border to the southern turned into mere hours. The clouds passed them by, drenching them solidly, making Natanael hold on tighter lest they slip from the slickness against the scales. Allonwë eventually relaxed against him, enjoying herself much more than he was in the moment, and wondered out loud what color personality he thought he might have.

"I don't understand the question," Natanael said.

"What's there to understand?" Noland asked. "Personally, I'm red."

"Oh, that's fitting," Allonwë said. "As for Nana, I think you're more of a cool blue or a silver."

"Blue's a good personality color," Noland nodded. "Loyal. Independent. Good for finding things."

"And Nana is the best tracker!" Allonwë said, clapping her hands together in pure joy. "I never have to worry about getting lost cause Nana will always find me."

Natanael flushed at the compliment, but tried to brush it off. "You don't exactly make it hard to find you, princess."

"Oh, but I have! Just to test you. And you found me every time," Allonwë replied. "You'll always find me, no matter what kind of trouble I get in to."

"Let's not make a habit of you getting into trouble, shall we?" Natanael pleaded.

Allonwë just laughed.

"Land just inside those trees, child," Noland called, getting their attention to the ground below.

Charlie circled a few times, getting lower and lower with each round until at last she touched down in the small clearing not a mile from where the trees ended and a great expanse of land opened up before them as a valley. Their voices fell silent as they grew closer to the edge of the forest, the sound of a group of people talking in the distance catching their attention. Natanael drew his sword silently, motioning for Allonwë to stay put and stay silent, but she refused, following him as quietly as she could, much to his dismay. Noland wasn't far behind. Charlie, however, stayed in the clearing because of her size and inability to maneuver through the trees quietly.

"This is the site," a familiar voice said, carrying upwards to the trees. Natanael, Noland, and Allonwë crawled to the edge and peered down into the valley. There, standing below them, were the three travelers and a new person who Allonwë recognized from the city from where she'd accidentally stolen her outfit. It was the person the travelers had given the bracelet to in the marketplace.

"Are you sure?" a female voice trailed up to them. It was the unidentified bracelet trader. "There's nothing out here."

"I feel it, General Keravuori," the Naga said in his drawl. "These undead bones o'mine can feel the dead beneath the earth."

"Poetic, General Haralambi," Keravuori muttered with disdain. "Did you bring the vials of the master's blood, or are you as useless to me as this information about your bones?"

"Aye, I brought it," the Naga said. So, it had a name. "You furies need to have some patience. The dead will rise soon enough. Since we need to make the seven points of the spell across the land with his blood, we'll take two vials a piece."

"I know how to do basic math, General Haralambi," Keravuori said flatly. "When we're done setting up the spell, you are to report back to the master before sunset. Understood? We only have a limited window of time for this to work."

"Aye, with the full moon tonight and all. Best time for spell work," Haralambi said slowly, as if considering something. "Wouldn't you agree, princess?"

The Naga looked up at Allonwë, Noland, and Natanael from where he stood and the two of them tried to duck back down and hide, but it was too late. They had been found out.

"Run!" Natanael whispered hoarsely.

The three elves scrambled to their feet and turned to run when a red-skinned creature landed before them, wings spread wide to help ease her descent. Her arms, which were a part of her wings, were feathered with brightly colored plumes that looked as if to be made of fire. She had talons for feet and was dressed in light armor that allowed her to move around freely.

When she landed before them, she pulled back a hood that hid her face and revealed strikingly beautiful features that mesmerized them for a moment, even in their fear of being caught by the undead Naga below. Her tail flickered back and forth, distracting Allonwë and breaking the spell that seemed to have fallen over her at the sight of the fury.

Turning to Natanael, she quickly slapped him across the face, distracting him, too.

"Ouch! What the hell Allonwë?" he asked.

"It's a glimmer spell!" she declared. "Slap Noland!"

Noland stood transfixed by the fury and hadn't moved despite their revealing conversation. It was as if he couldn't hear them. Natanael slapped him, and the old elf instinctively slapped him back, blinking himself into the present.

"Ouch!" Natanael swore under his breath. "It's a glimmer spell!" he explained to Noland, who looked ready for a fight.

Dawning flashed across Noland's face and he shook his head. "Good work! We have to keep from looking her in the eye as we fight or we'll be caught in her spell again!"

Keravuori drew her a sword from her back and grinned maliciously at Natanael, who held his own in a practiced position, ready to fight. She lunged first, and he parried, striking hard and fast against her swing and throwing it off balance. She turned the momentum into a whirl and swung in a circle, coming at him from the other side. Natanael barely had time to dodge backwards as he kept forcing himself not to look into her face as he fought.

"Spread the blood!" she screeched over Natanael's shoulder. "I'll take care of them!"

"Charlie!" Allonwë screamed. "Help us!"

Off in the distance they could hear the thunderous roar of a dragon, and the fury general narrowed her eyes at Allonwë with a feral hiss. Natanael swung his sword at Keravuori, getting her attention away from the princess and back onto him before she could think to attack Allonwë. Swords clashed again, once, twice, thrice in quick procession as they tried to knock each other's weapon from the other's hands.

Natanael's were aching with the effort to keep his hands on his hilt as he chopped and swung and thrust his way through the fight, the effort to keep up with the fury slowing him down. He watched her feet rather than her face for any sign of movement before she would strike, and so far, it hadn't steered him wrong. She would shift her weight through the stances much like that of a dance, and not for the first time, he wondered if this was just child's play to her.

She was distracting them from the actual issue: the undead travelers.

"Allonwë!" Natanael called as he pushed the fury back with all the force he could muster. "Send Charlie after the others!"

"But you need help!" Allonwë argued.

"I can handle this. We need to stop their plan!" he grunted between strikes.

Sparks flew from the metal as the swords clashed and the

fury didn't seem to be tiring anytime soon. She rushed at Natanael, who met her sword hilt to hilt and used her momentum to throw her away from Allonwë. Noland rushed out of the way in fear of being sliced to death by their weapons, and narrowly escaped losing most of one of his long, long ears.

"Charlie!" Allonwë called again, running through the forest to meet the dragon half way.

Charlie was having trouble landing in the woods, and ended up knocking over a couple of trees trying to get to Allonwë.

"Allonwë!" Charlie called, lowering her head down into the copse of trees to reach the princess.

"The undead travelers! They're over that ridge! We gotta stop them!" Allonwë said urgently. "They're setting up some kind of spell. I-I don't know what, but I think it's got something to do with necromancy!"

Charlie gasped and looked in the direction of the valley. "Stay here!" Charlie demanded.

"I want to come with you. I want to help!" Allonwë balked.

Charlie shook her head. "We need you to stay safe. I need you to stay safe. You're my friend. I can't lose you. I just met you."

The sound of swords clashing distracted Charlie for an instant. She looked back at Allonwë.

"Promise me you'll be safe," Charlie insisted.

"Okay," Allonwë said hesitantly. "I promise." Her heart hammered in her chest as she looked around for anything she could use to level the playing field. But the only magic she knew was small things. Like how to start a fire or mend holes in clothing. Her education had failed her.

Or had it? She noted some twigs and sticks on the ground and started gathering them together in order to bundle them up. She grabbed some vines from the underbrush, trying to ignore their thorns tearing into her fingers as she wrapped them around the bundle to keep it together. Whispering the igniting words to start the fire, Allonwë blew on the sticks as they started smoking. Suddenly they burst into flame in her hands and she had to jerk her face back lest her eyebrows be singed off.

"Hey ugly!" she called, running back towards the fury. "Take this!" she declared, smacking the fury on top of the head with the flaming monstrosity she'd created. The resounding *smack!* as her head connected with the sticks was enough to make Natanael wince. The fury's hair caught fire, and she screamed, dropping her sword and patting her head to keep the flames from burning her further. Natanael took advantage of her distraction and impaled her with his sword just as the last of the flames were put out. Keravuori doubled over in pain as he kicked her off the end of his blade with the flat of his boot and sent her sprawling in the dirt.

"Are you crazy?" Natanael said, not for the first time. "What is it with you and jumping into danger to help me?"

"It worked, didn't it?" Allonwë said, trying to catch her breath. Her blood was still pumping with adrenaline. She'd helped!

"Screw this!" Keravuori declared, getting to her feet and growling with pure hatred in her voice. "I'm through dealing with pesky elves!"

She threw her sword at Natanael, who had to dive out of the way and into the dirt to avoid being sliced in half by it. She ran at Allonwë, punching her so hard in the face that the princess blacked out and had to be caught by Keravuori. Grappling the princess in her talons, she muttered a magic word before launching them both into the air with a speed and height that should have been impossible with their combined weight.

"Allonwë!" Natanael screamed, scrambling to his feet.

But it was too late.

Meanwhile, in the field below, Charlie was setting everything on fire. The three travelers had dumped five out of the seven vials by the time Charlie had caught up with them, their speed aided by wings for the other two and magic for the Naga. When the second traveler fell to dragon fire for the second time, he didn't get back up. And Charlie had discovered their secret: they had to be killed twice to stay dead.

The Naga was running away from her across the field at an alarming rate, vial in hand as he uncorked the glass and dove for the last remaining spot that needed to be coated with blood, when Charlie took a deep breath and let out a stream of fire that stretched across the field and charred the creature to its timely death.

But not before it spilled the vial across the ground, shattering it beneath its weight as it fell.

The Naga melted into a pile of boiling mud that wreaked of death and decay, and Charlie could smell it even as far away as she was from it. They all stank like that when they died. Of unnaturalness. Wrongness. Evil.

When she stood and looked back at the others, Charlie heard Natanael scream Allonwë's name, and looked up in the air in the direction he was staring, but only saw endless cloud cover as a storm brewed overhead. The heat rising from the valley wasn't helping as the sound of thunder boomed overhead, the cool wind currents clashing with the heat of dragon fire.

Launching into the air and gliding over to the edge of the valley where they were, she saw Noland was all but pulling his hair out. He looked almost as distraught as Natanael did.

"This isn't good!" Noland was chanting. "No! No! No!"

"We have to follow them. We have to get her back!" Natanael said. "Charlie, can you fly us?"

"Yes, but where?" the dragon asked.

"No! You don't understand! He has her now! There is no hope!" Noland was saying.

Natanael grabbed him by the shirt and got in his face. "I will not let my charge be stolen by some fury and taken to gods knows where without trying my damnedest to find her!"

"You don't understand!" Noland said again. "He has her blood now! The spell is complete! Tonight, when the full moon rises, so will the undead and now that he has the weapon, there will be no stopping him! We have to leave the country before it's too late!"

"Coward!" Natanael growled, throwing Noland to the ground. "I will not abandon her when she needs me!"

"You don't get it, do you? There's nothing that can stop him now that he's got her blood to activate it! It protects against everything - Elven magic, dragon magic, dwarven magic, you name it! He's going to kill her, raise her from the dead, and use her as his minion to take over the throne of Kutawë and march upon the rest of the world!" Noland raved.

"Then all the more reason to go after her!" Natanael argued.

"You can't stop him. I tried! Thousands of years ago, I tried! I thought I killed him, but he came back!" Noland warned.

"Who, Old Elf?" Charlie asked, not following this story. "Who has Allonwë?"

Noland looked at her, wild-eyed. "The necromancer of Jeshirir. Sheldane, my brother."

Lesson 9

THEM BONES THEM BONES GONNA WALK AROUND

"Your *what*?" Natanael demanded, turning back on Noland like he was about to strike him down where he stood. As if it were his fault Allonwë had been captured and flown away to who knew where. In fact, he wasn't entirely sure that it wasn't his fault now.

"My brother," Noland repeated. "Can't you hear?"

"Old elf, I'm about this close to skewering you if you don't start explaining everything so I can get my princess back," Natanael said darkly.

"They adopted him into the royal family when they thought they couldn't conceive," Noland began speaking quickly. "He was raised to be the next king. The next ruler of Kutawë. Then our mother became pregnant with me, and when I was born, there was a great debate about who would get the throne. In the end... they gave it to me because of my bloodline."

"What became of your brother?" Natanael asked.

"He became my adviser. My right-hand man. I trusted him with everything," Noland said, a growl in his voice.

"What happened?" Charlie asked.

Noland's face went slack with grief as his mind seemed to flash back to those memories.

"There was a skirmish at the border of the Elf and Dragon lands. They killed thousands of elves in a single night. The children that had escaped couldn't understand what happened. They were so young. Just... babies they were. Toddlers. How they escaped, I never found out. They knew something was wrong. Something had taken their families away from them. And they'd found the nearest village by mere accident. The villagers brought them to us, but we couldn't gain any kind of knowledge about what happened to them. So Sheldane went out with his men to discover what happened. And when he came back, he said the dragons had attacked and burned the whole town to the ground."

"But dragons are peaceful!" Charlie balked, on the verge of tears judging from the emotions in her voice.

"I was hot-blooded. Stupid. I believed him," Noland said. "He was my brother, why wouldn't I? My right-hand man. Why would he lie about this? I never thought to question him."

Noland hung his head.

"It wasn't until three wars had come and passed, all my doing, that I found out he was using me to build an army of the dead to rise against the armies of Kutawë, and march upon Sitani castle. I found out the day his armies had us surrounded in the middle of the last war with the dragons. He did it to weaken us... to split our attention between the undead soldiers and the dragons who were defending their borders with a vengeance. I summoned the mages of Barlow to help defend against such evil magic, but Sheldane was an archmage. And a powerful one at that. It took everything they had to decimate his armies. Then the Elder Dragon came to fight, seeing the opportunity that we were weakened. He wanted to end the battle once and for all. I don't blame him now. But then, I was still stupid. I could have called for a truce. Could have turned my brother over to them for punishment for his crimes against both nations. But I fought for all I was worth against the Great Dragon. He wanted the Heart Stone I used as my weapon. The soul stone of his mate."

"Sister," Charlie whispered.

"Yes," Noland nodded. "I slayed him, thinking it was the only way I could save my country. But Sheldane would not be stopped there. He came after me on the battlefield and we fought till the death. He couldn't touch me, for the Heart Stone protected me. I eventually dealt the final blow that took him out, and when the dust settled, I was nowhere near the heart of the battle any more. I threw off the gauntlet that had the Heart Stone in it. And I ran from the battle, having lost my closest friend, ally, and brother, killed by my very hands. He may have turned out to be my enemy, but he never started out that way. He'd been my confidant. My wing man when I met my wife. I lost her in childbirth to our daughter, whom I left the throne to in the end. I told her before the eve of battle that day that the line would continue through the female line. Through her. For she was strong and wise and brave. More so than I ever was."

"What happened after you ran away?" Charlie asked.

"The two sides called a truce," Natanael cut in. "And we've not fought since."

"And you?" Charlie asked Noland.

"I lost my mind. I became a hermit. Lost track of time. Probably hit my head too hard in the last battle. I became suspicious of the world and everyone around me. Until the day I met you," Noland said, looking up at Charlie. "And you taught me that there was still some good in this world, even if I didn't deserve it."

"You're right, you didn't deserve it," Charlie replied. "You should have gone to the village yourself and you would have seen that no dragon fire had burned down that village. I remember the stories. The undead burned that village down.

The dragons drove them from our land when they tried to cross the border. That's when your precious brother told you we attacked."

Noland's head still hung in shame. "I can never repay the world for my transgressions."

"But that doesn't mean you should stop trying," Natanael replied. "You don't have to complete the action of saving the world, but you don't have the luxury of leaving it to die, either."

"I suppose you're right," Noland said slowly. He got back to his feet and dusted himself off. "Let's go save your princess."

～

Startling awake with a gasp, Allonwë jumped into a sitting position before groaning in pain as her face throbbed sharply. She muttered something under her breath about the pain, gingerly touching the cheek the fury had punched with her fingertips.

"That looks like it hurts," an unfamiliar voice said.

Allonwë jumped again, looking around the dark room - cave? Cave. - where there, in the shadows, was a scrawny-looking figure wearing tattered robes. He had pitch black hair that fell to his shoulders like a midnight waterfall, and eyes that could pierce her soul. They were reddish brown in hue with gold flecks that gave them an eerie look.

"I'm sorry, I didn't mean to startle you," he said, his deep voice carrying well in the space even though he spoke quietly. His tone was calming despite their situation. Allonwë got the feeling he'd been here a while. Perhaps they were both prisoners.

"It's fine," Allonwë said. "I've just been in a fight and was sort of expecting to see them reappear." She examined the wall suspiciously around her, as if expecting them to melt out of it at some point.

"Ah, I see," the man said. She noted his ears, which were unnaturally long for a human's, were rounded at the tips with scars that made them look docked elf ears. Who was this guy?

"Who are you?" she asked blatantly.

"My name is Sheldane," he replied.

The name didn't ring any bells for Allonwë in particular, but something about it sounded interesting to her.

"Sheldaaane... Shell-dane. Sheeeeldane. Hm," she hummed, testing out his name. "Interesting. I'm Allonwë."

"Allonwë," he greeted. "What a strong name."

"Thanks," Allonwë said. *I think.* "How long was I out?"

"Not long," Sheldane reassured her. "You have missed nothing exciting... yet."

"Exciting? Like what?" Allonwë asked.

"The Archmage is going to perform a spell tonight, I hear," Sheldane said. "A very special one that will bless the land for the millennium to come."

"Oh," Allonwë said, taken back. Then she remembered the undead in the clearing. "We gotta warn the Archmage someone is trying to sabotage his spell!"

"Oh? Who would that be?" Sheldane asked curiously.

"Three undead travelers that have been chasing me all over the country!" Allonwë replied. "They're trying to aid the necromancer into raising an army of the undead! Who knows what kind of havoc they're going to unleash!"

"Oh, my!" Sheldane commented. "That would be treacherous. We should do something about that."

"Where's the Archmage?" Allonwë asked, getting to her feet and looking around. She needed to figure out where she was and how to get out of here. What was it with finding herself in caves recently? Well, the last one she met Charlie in, so perhaps they weren't all that bad. This one didn't have any kind of treasure lying around, so it probably wasn't another dragon's den. Was it dwarven, perhaps? Or maybe goblin? She hoped it wasn't goblin in manner. Those things would eat anything. And she was included in that list.

"You're speaking to him," Sheldane replied simply.

"You're the archmage?" she asked, blinking in surprise. "That's great! You can get us out of here!"

"Hm," Sheldane hummed, considering her statement. "I could. But then I wouldn't be at the perfect place to perform my spell on the land."

"Don't you get it?" Allonwë demanded. "This necromancer is probably going to kill thousands of people if we don't stop them!"

"What makes you think that?" Sheldane asked. "Has he said he's going to kill anyone?"

"Well... no," Allonwë said, taken aback by the statement. "But his minions tried to kill my Nana, and anyone who tries to hurt Nana is a villain in my book."

"They tried to kill your grandmother?" Sheldane asked, shocked for the first time.

"No, Nana is my bodyguard," Allonwë replied, confusing him further. "It's short for Natanael."

"Ah," Sheldane said. "That makes much more sense. You see, you are needed for this spell. That's one of the reasons why you've been brought here today. And probably why they tried to kill your bodyguard if he was hindering you from being brought here."

"Wait, I thought the necromancer wanted me for something. You said you were an archmage," Allonwë said. This time, it was her turn to be confused.

"No, you're right. I'm an archmage," nodded Sheldane. "Aaand a necromancer."

Allonwë stared at him for a long moment before turning on heel and running as fast as she could in any direction that wasn't towards him. All she could think of was to get out of there as soon as she could before whatever this spell he had planned for her could take effect.

"Keravuori," Sheldane said plainly.

The fury from before flew down from somewhere high above Allonwë, landing before her and blocking her way. Allonwë darted back a few steps, glancing up to see where she had been perched, and noticed a hole in the cave's roof that was letting in moonlight.

Wherever she was, however long she'd been there, it had given the moon time to rise to its near zenith in the sky, almost directly above the hole in the cave's ceiling. Looking back at the fury, Allonwë noticed the very thing for which she was looking.

There, behind the winged woman, was the entry to the cave. Glancing around, she noticed there was a rock formation directly beneath the hole in the ceiling and for a moment Allonwë wondered if they were going to sacrifice her like a lamb to the gods.

She needed to buy time.

"I, uh," she said, looking between Sheldane and Keravuori. "I don't suppose you know what color personality you are? I mean, if we're going to be spending some time together, we should get to know each other first, right?"

"...How hard did I hit you?" the general asked, blinking at her. "She can still be used if I scrambled her mind, right?" she asked over Allonwë's shoulder to Sheldane.

"All we need is her blood. She can be as stupid as Haralambi for all I care, so long as we have her blood," Sheldane replied flatly. "Don't let her get away like he did."

"Nana!" Allonwë shrieked.

"Call for your grandmother all you want. She isn't here to save you, little princess," Keravuori said with a sadistic smile.

"He's my bodyguard!" Allonwë yelled. "Nanaaaaa!"

"Stop yelling, you annoying little elf!" Keravuori hissed. "Or I'll make sure this hurts a lot!"

"NO!" Allonwë yelled, calling for Natanael once again.

She ran across the cave away from the fury, slowing only long enough to pick up a rock and throw it at the creature, following her at a determined pace. The rock bounced off her head and made her curse.

"You're beginning to be more trouble than you're worth!" Keravuori growled, irritated as she launched forward, wings spread and dove for Allonwë.

"Yeah?" Allonwë said, running in a zig-zag pattern that threw off Keravuori's trajectory. "Well, your buddies said the same thing and look where that got them? Re-dead!"

"It's just dead," Sheldane called, watching her run across the cave from his spot, leaning against the wall. "Not re-dead."

"Oh," Allonwë said, picking up another rock and pelting Keravuori with it. "Well, they're dead again, is what I'm trying to say. They were dead, then you raised them from the dead and they were undead. Now they're dead-dead again."

"Right, no, I understood what you meant," Sheldane said, nodding. "Do you mind holding still for this? You're giving me a headache calling for your body guard so much."

"Actually, I do mind," Allonwë replied, screaming even louder for Natanael to come. "I'm tired of being chased by bloody chickens! Come save me!"

"What did you just call me?" Keravuori shouted. "Why you little-" She lunged and tackled Allonwë to the ground. Allonwë rolled onto her back and Keravuori started scratching at her face, screeching like a barn owl as she did so. "Call me a chicken! I'll claw your eyes out! Don't need your eyes for this!"

Allonwë caught her fists and locked their fingers together, trying to unbalance Keravuori and topple her. Allonwë let out an ear-piercing scream to throw the fury off her game, but only ticked her off even further. Head butting Allonwë in the forehead, Keravuori caused the princess pass out cold. When she came to, they tied her up and laid on the altar beneath the full moon, mouth stuffed full of what felt like a dirty rag.

"Don't roll," Sheldane warned. "That fall will hurt."

Allonwë tried to reply, "Gee, thanks for your concern!" but it came out garbled.

"Of course. I care about all of my sacrifices, living dead soldiers, and companions. It's what makes me a good leader," he replied, coming into view while polishing a knife. "I care about the individual and the masses."

"Excuse me?" Allonwë garbled. "How is making undead caring?"

"Sorry I didn't catch that," Sheldane said. "You've got too much rag in your mouth."

"How is killing people and making them undead caring?" Allonwë tried again.

"Still didn't get it," Sheldane replied, shaking his head. "But I don't think it was very nice regarding the living dead. That's a much more politically correct term than undead. See, the undead just reduces them to corpses with no will of their own. And I assure you, my necromancy is much kinder than that. They still hold their original personalities and will power when I resurrect them. There are spells that are inhumane to the living dead that strip them of their will power and make them pawns to be used at the necromancer's discrepancy, but that's not fair, I don't think. Even in death, they deserve respect and autonomy."

Allonwë asked something very un-princess like that equated to "What in the world?" but with some dwarven swear words thrown in for good measure. Her throat was hurting from all the screaming she'd done, but she still felt like she had a few more in her should he come any closer to her with that knife. Surely, Natanael was getting closer to finding her. Surely he would get here soon enough and rescue her. He was probably worried sick.

"Oh, but that's not to say you'll have autonomy when I kill you," Sheldane admitted and Allonwë's heart skipped in her chest. "See, I need you to follow my will. It pains me to have to do that to you, because I believe the living dead should have their own lives and willpower to an extent. You know, aside from creating more war and whatnot. But then again, you can't have bloodshed if there's no more blood left to shed. But for this plan to work, your..." He squinted at her. "Spunk, if you will, will have to be reined in. I apologize for having to do this while you're still alive. It's part of the minion spell and all."

"Nanaaaa!" Allonwë yelled through the rag.

"There you go again," Sheldane sighed. "You will not be rescued. I'm about to free your soul from your body, then reattach it by carving a sigil into your skin. Now, where do you want your soul tattoo to be? This can be very telling about a person's personality. You mentioned wanting to know more about those earlier. So where will it be? Chest? Face? Hand? Thigh? Back? The possibilities are nearly endless."

He had to be nearby. He had to hear her. With Noland's ears being as long as they were, one of them had to hear her. Charlie had to smell her from wherever they were. They had to be following some kind of trail. And she was going to make sure they could hear her and pinpoint her location, if nothing else, through screaming alone.

"Help me!" she cried, pulling at her bonds as she tried to free herself.

Tears streamed down her face as the fear took over. What if they didn't find her? Her heart was pounding in her chest, sweat forming on her brow. Sheldane was getting closer with his knife, and reached out with his free hand, putting it on her forehead.

"Shhh," he said, as if trying to calm a small child. "This won't hurt. Keravuori was just being mean. My magic will numb the area so you don't feel a thing. Now, do you have a preference? I can put it somewhere visible, or somewhere it'll be hidden."

Allonwë shook her head violently, as if trying to tell him no, but really, she just wanted his hand off her forehead.

"Alright," Sheldane said calmly. "I'll put it on your back. That way, you don't have to look at it if you don't want to." He turned to the side and motioned for Keravuori to come forward. "Come. Flip her over."

Keravuori stepped forward, uncrossing her arms and grabbing the struggling princess, and flipping her over onto her stomach. She began wriggling in place as if to make it more difficult for him to get a purchase on her skin with the knife.

"Hold her still," Sheldane instructed and Keravuori's knee went into the small of her back and she held Allonwë down with her hands and talons.

Allonwë struggled and tried her damnedest to get away, but she felt him pull the belt off her waist and flip the fabric of her shirt over the top of her head so he had access to her full back, and the cold steel pressed into her skin on her shoulder blade.

She screamed despite feeling no pain, as he promised. She felt the knife make precision movements quickly and effortlessly, as if by a practiced hand. Allonwë continued to scream, begging him to stop and to let her go, but Sheldane ignored her. Sobbing, she called for Natanael to rescue her. To please, please find her again. He could always find her. He could always save her in the nick of time.

But this time, Natanael didn't come.

And this time she'd gotten far, far in over her head. She begged to be released. To stop having him carve the intricate sigil into her back. But it went on for what seemed like ages. The cold metal became warm against her from the blood pouring from the open wound and against the steel. And yet he still worked. The sigil spanned from her shoulder blade and expanded to the middle of her back. She tried to buck against the restraints and Keravuori to mess it up somehow, but it was like they set her in stone. She couldn't budge. Couldn't resist. Couldn't do anything but scream and cry.

I don't want to die, she thought. *Not here. Not like this. Please! Nana!*

Even so, Natanael didn't come. Her throat constricted as she felt the knife go deep into her skin. She coughed and shuddered, but Sheldane just whispered to her that everything was alright and that she was doing great as if she weren't having living death carved into her body. There was no coming back from this. No escaping this. She was just going to die here in this cave, all because she wanted to play hide and scare with Natanael instead of doing her studies like she should have been.

Natanael would not find her this time. And it was all her fault. She'd finally gone where he couldn't follow, and her journey into the depths of the five hells wasn't over yet.

There was a small jab against her back as he seemed to put the final touches on her sigil and suddenly the pressure against her back ceased. She heard Sheldane speaking in a low, muttering tone, and her skin prickled everywhere he'd carved.

"There," he said. "Got you all healed up. That scarred nicely."

Allonwë's voice was hoarse as she lay there, bare and feeling exposed, sobbing quietly. She was going to die here. She was going to be killed, then resurrected, and forced to march on her family's castle. Would she be coherent like the undead travelers had been? Would she get home and be fussed over, only to bring her family's ruin from the inside? Or would she be mindless and destroy everything in her wake without mercy?

She didn't like the idea of either, but she'd rather be mindless than lull her family into a false sense of security before killing them. Sure, she always complained about them, but her father would always sneak her treats whenever she and her mother had a fight.

Her mother, despite not listening to her complaints most of the time, let her study things she had interests in, however fleeting that interest turned out to be, on top of her regular studies. She'd always been an advocate of learning, regardless of how big or how little the special interest turned out to be.

She wanted to see their faces again, and hug them and have them tell her she was going to be alright. That all this was just a horrible nightmare and that it would all go away.

But it wasn't. And they wouldn't. And she couldn't.

And she would never see Natanael again.

It was all over now.

"Now," Sheldane said, letting Keravuori get off her. "Let's get you fixed back up."

They pulled her shirt back down and fastened the belt back around her waist. Her sides heaved with sobs as they worked.

I want to go home, she thought, squeezing her eyes shut.

"Now the fun part begins," Sheldane said. "You get to watch me raise the dead before we start on you."

"You're not going to kill me now?" Allonwë asked around the rag in her mouth.

"Where would the fun be in that?" Sheldane asked. "I like to have an audience when I work. The moon is almost at its zenith. It's time to get to work."

Keravuori dragged Allonwë to her feet, unchaining her bonds from the altar. Allonwë looked back and saw the blood smeared there on the rock, and looked up at the light of the moon spilling through the hole in the cave roof.

Sheldane led her to the mouth of the cave where Allonwë looked around curiously, only to have her heart leap into her throat at the sight of the drop off there into the valley below. The only way up here was through flight. If she had run out of the cave opening, she would have fallen to her death. They were in the mountains somewhere. This was more like a balcony without a railing than it was a cave opening. Maybe this was an unfinished dwarf cave.

The necromancer muttered words in a language Allonwë didn't recognize. His eyes glowed, his finger tips pulsed with magic that surged down into the stone beneath their feet, and suddenly thunder cracked overhead, though the skies were clear.

Only it wasn't thunder, Allonwë realized. It was the sound of the earth shaking as things from beneath it began to rise up. The ground cracked and shook and gave way to the bones and corpses beneath it. Ones that had been lost to time and forgotten. Ones that had been buried on the field of battle because there were too many to take back home.

Keravuori held onto Allonwë's bonds from behind as they watched the dead begin to rise and form of block formations below. They were all elves, from the looks of it. No dragons, thank the gods.

"Impressive isn't it?" Sheldane asked, smiling at the look on her face. "And now the finishing touch," he said, reaching into his pocket in his robes and pulling out the bracelet that had started this whole mess. He turned to Allonwë and smiled. "Now, my dear, it's your turn to take the stage."

Allonwë took a step back, swallowing hard as she bumped into Keravuori.

"I need your blood to activate this bracelet," he continued. "Unfortunately, it has to be somewhat living blood and driven by command, otherwise you could stay alive for this part."

"What if I just promise to give you the throne and you let me go, and we never have to see each other again?" she asked.

"Take the rag from her mouth," he instructed.

The fury did so, and Allonwë repeated the question.

"I'm afraid there's still the matter of your parents being in the way," Sheldane replied. "And their armies. But with you being my secret weapon, I'll be able to wipe them out without issue by resurrecting the dragons, then resurrect your parents and their armies so that they can live peaceful lives under my rule. It'll be a win-win."

"What if I just do what you tell me to do, and talk them into giving you the throne rather than killing everyone?" Allonwë bargained again. "We could just give me the bracelet, resurrect the dragons, and make it so that you have your undead army to make them stand down. I'm sure they'd listen to you more if I were still alive than if I were dead. Think about it. I'm worth more to you alive than I am dead."

"You're really not," Sheldane said, shaking his head. "I can control the dead when necessary. I can't control the living. They're just so... unruly. And I'm afraid I can't trust you to do my bidding should I hand this over. It nearly got me killed once, and it took me years to rebuild my strength and magic. I'll not let that happen again."

Allonwë tried to open her mouth to bargain some more and try to convince him she would listen to him if he let her and her family go, but he held up a hand and stopped her.

"I've heard enough. Now, don't worry, I'll make this as painless as the sigil was," he declared, stepping forward.

"Nana!" Allonwë screamed again, trying to break free of Keravuori's grasp. Keravuori grabbed the back of Allonwë's hair and held her still as Sheldane positioned the knife between two of her ribs, right above her heart, which was hammering in her chest like a hummingbird trying to escape a cage.

Thunder clapped behind him as Sheldane stepped forward, but this time he stopped, turning to look. It hadn't been his magic that had made that noise, despite the shaking of the mountain beneath their feet. It had been the sound of a dragon's talons clashing into the side of the cliff face, as Charlie's head appeared inside the cave opening, Natanael and Noland riding on her back. Charlie let out a roar that had Sheldane covering his docked ears.

"He's going to kill me!" Allonwë shrieked, her voice straining with the effort. She tasted copper in the back of her throat and wondered if she had irritated her skin to the point of bleeding. She didn't care. Nana had found her just like he always did and the world was about to right itself.

"Let her go," Natanael said, jumping off Charlie's back and into the cave. His sword was drawn and at the ready, and Keravuori hissed, pulling Allonwë back a few steps.

"Brother!" Noland called. "Stop this madness."

"Noland!" Sheldane hissed. "I thought I killed you in the last war!"

Suddenly, Sheldane's quiet demeanor changed into one of pure rage. "How dare you show your face again after everything you did to me! I will kill you where you stand and this time I'm going to make sure you can't come back ever again!"

"Sheldane, please!" Noland tried to reason. "Don't make this harder than it has to be. You can still stop this madness."

"Madness?" Sheldane spat. "I'm the only reasonable one here! All I want is peace in the world and the living are doing everything in their power to prevent that from happening. People are bloodthirsty warmongers. At least when I kill something, I have the audacity to give it a second chance at life!"

"That's rich coming from someone trying to murder thousands in order to take the throne!" Natanael growled.

"Is that what you think this is?" Sheldane asked. "A grab for power? No child. I am trying to bring peace to the world through necromancy. By making them living dead, they will have free will, yes, but I can keep them from being upstarts and warmongers at the same time. People will die, but they won't stay dead for long. I will raise everyone from the dead with the intent of living as one. We will nourish the world back to its former glory! Not this cesspit of cruelty that it is now!"

"You're insane! That's not free will, that's your will!" Natanael spat. "If you really want peace, then negotiate it without the threat of death and we'll listen."

"I tried that. For years as the adviser to the king! But did anyone listen? NO! They wanted to expand borders and steal lands from others. They wanted to have more power so that the other races couldn't take what should never have been theirs to begin with! I tried to do things your way. I did everything in my power and was tossed aside. So, I took things into my own hands. But then YOU had to ruin things with your weapon!" Sheldane declared angrily, jabbing a finger in Noland's direction. "You couldn't leave well enough alone! You wanted the power of the dragons too! Well, now I'm taking that power from you. I'm taking it and raising their dead so I can reunite them with their families! And nothing can stop me!"

Sheldane turned and raised a knife at Allonwë's chest, preparing to bring down the strike and kill her, but Natanael's sword cut off his hand before he ever had the chance.

Screaming in pain and growling a healing spell through clenched teeth, the nub where the hand once was began glowing with the same light as his eyes, as magic pulsed from it and stopped the bleeding. The knife and bracelet clattered to the ground, and Keravuori's grip on Allonwë lessened as she dove for Natanael. Only she dove straight into the thrust of his sword, sending her sprawling onto the floor, clutching her midsection in pain.

Sheldane was scrabbling for the knife with his remaining hand. "I'll kill you and make sure you never come back!" he growled, bringing the knife down and piercing Natanael's shoulder through the armor. Natanael crashed into the cave wall and slid down it from the blow, and Sheldane began performing a spell over him.

"NO!" Allonwë shrieked. She snatched up the bracelet and put it on her wrist. She ran to Sheldane and grabbed handfuls of his robes, and spun him away from Natanael and into the depths of the cave where he rolled across the floor, having tripped over his own feet. "Charlie" she yelled. "Light this bitch up!"

She marched over to Sheldane as Charlie took a deep breath, fires lighting up her chest, and grabbed him by the front of his robes, getting into his face.

"No one. Hurts. My. Nana," she declared. Charlie let loose the fire and it bathed over Allonwë and Sheldane like waves crashing on a beach.

The heat was so intense, Sheldane's body burst into flame, his screams echoing throughout the cavernous area. His hand grabbed onto Allonwë's, trying to break free of her grasp, but he couldn't gain purchase as it melted away his fingers to the bone. He watched her stare him down in anger, until his eyes boiled in his skull and he went blind, the last image of her untouched by the fire as red as her hair as it devoured him to his core.

His magic pulsed as it tried to heal him as the flames continuously peeled away at his flesh, scarring, marring, and deforming his body. At last, his bones fell to the ground, his screams having died away, and disintegrated into a chunky dust filled with bone fragments that the heat couldn't quite destroy. They glowed with the fire, cracking and breaking into smaller pieces as Charlie's breath petered out.

"Allonwë!" Natanael's screams were finally reaching her ears.

As the flames died down around her, she looked back at Natanael, who stared at her in horror. The fear on his face was palpable, the terror in his eyes as she stood there unharmed making her heart hurt. She gave him a small smile and held up her wrist where she'd placed the bracelet.

"Sometimes you just gotta have the right accessories to win a fight," she managed, before collapsing to her knees, shaking. She really had just done that. Watched a man - an elf - burn to death before her very eyes.

But Natanael had found her, and now he was safe.

"Allonwë," Charlie called. "Are you hurt?"

"No," the princess replied shakily. "But Nana is. Can you heal him?"

"He needs to come over here so I can reach him. I can't get into the cave. The opening is too small," Charlie said.

"I'll bring him over," Allonwë said, struggling to get to her feet. She made her way over to Natanael and helped him remove the dagger, which hadn't gone as far into him as she'd originally thought because of his armor blocking most of the blow, and got him to his feet with lots of grunting and swearing.

"You're the most... insane elf I've ever met!" Natanael declared, hugging her. A thrill went through her at the contact. "How did you know that would work?" He asked, taking her face in his hands and examining her for any injuries.

She didn't want to think about the scars on her back.

"I didn't," Allonwë admitted. "I just knew I couldn't let him live."

Natanael put his forehead to hers and she relished in the comfort of his touch.

"Promise me you'll never do that again," Natanael pleaded, closing his eyes.

"I can't do it again," she smiled with a giggle. "I have to give Charlie back her sister."

"Thank you, Allonwë," the dragon said softly.

"Of course," the elf princess replied. "Now, let's get Nana healed up and see about dealing with the armies of the undead."

"No need," Noland said, pointing out into the field where all the bodies had disintegrated too. "They fell apart with Sheldane's demise."

POSSUMS AREN'T THE ONLY THINGS THAT PLAY DEAD

H ealing Natanael didn't take long. Once he was patched up, they all three piled onto Charlie's back and flew out of the cave and off the side of the mountain to land in the valley below. Once on the ground, they dismounted and looked around the area. There were bodies strewn about in various levels of decay. The stench was horrible and Allonwë lost what little contents she had in her stomach from the overwhelming presence of it.

"This is so creepy," she shivered, wiping her mouth and wrapping her arms around herself. "Let's just go..."

"We need to make sure they're going to stay dead," Natanael said, drawing his sword, scabbard and all, off his belt. He poked one body with the sheathed end of his sword, feeling like it would just be rude to the dead to go around poking them with the sharp end if they were, in fact, dead, all whilst waiting for it to jerk awake again. "Can't have these things attacking Sitani castle just when we think it's safe-"

Allonwë felt something move under her foot and screamed, "They're alive!" or at least tried to. It more or less came out as a scream that caused Natanael to whirl around, trying to draw his sword. The scabbard flew off and hit

Noland in the face, who fell to the ground, causing a disembodied head to fly up and into Allonwë's outstretched arms that were reaching for Natanael, only to catch the gaping maw of a soldier long dead. She screamed again and Charlie blew fire over her to incinerate the head. Thankfully, Allonwë had yet to take off the bracelet, and it had resulted in no injury to her, merely flakes of undead being breathed over her.

"Stop that!" Natanael scolded Charlie. "You're going to give me a heart attack! Or blow us to bits."

"You?" Allonwë argued. "I'm the one that stepped on the undead and ticked it off before I was forced to hold its head!"

"That was my tail," Charlie said. "You stepped on it and scared me."

"Oh," Allonwë said. "Sorry."

"It's okay," Charlie replied.

"Can someone help me up?" Noland asked.

Natanael helped him to his feet once he re-sheathed his sword and stored it back on his belt. They looked around in silence, then glanced back up the mountain where the cave entrance was. There was still smoke coming from inside from the burning of the necromancer.

"This is just creepy," Allonwë repeated. "Let's go home."

"I did it," Noland breathed. "I lived through the apocalypse."

"Yeah, thanks for helping back there," Allonwë said sarcastically.

"I tried to talk him down," Noland said. "But as always, he never listened."

"Maybe you should have listened to him more in the first place and we could have avoided all this," Allonwë said.

"Allonwë," Natanael said. "It's over. We just need to go home now."

"He's walking," Charlie declared. "Now that we don't need him anymore and I have my sister back, I'm not carrying him a step further."

"Fair enough," Allonwë nodded. "I will not make you either. It was creepy enough, having to be carved like a pig on a feast day by a guy with docked ears. I don't want to deal with your ears flapping in the wind again. They make the weirdest noise."

"Wait, my brother carved a sigil into you?" Noland asked urgently.

"I'm sorry your what?" Allonwë demanded.

"That was your great, great, great, great whatever uncle, the Archmage and Necromancer, Sheldane of Jeshirir," Natanael replied.

"I'm sorry when was that going to be brought up because I feel like that was an important tidbit," Allonwë said, looking horrified. "I just killed my own family. Granted, he killed thousands of people back in his day."

"He was adopted," Noland said. "There was no blood relation."

"Adoption just means they chose you and you found your family, not that you are someone who should be cast aside as 'oh well, he's not like the rest of us because he doesn't share the same blood'. No, you raised him to be what he was. You entertained the thought of him being the king, then ripped that away from him. There's more to this than a grab for power, Noland. He gave the dead autonomy over their bodies. I saw it firsthand with the travelers." Natanael said.

"And me when he tried to let me choose where to put the sigil..." Allonwë's voice trailed off as she considered something.

"I just thought he wanted me dead," Noland said. "You heard his plans! He wanted to raise an army of the undead and take over the world! How is that not evil?"

"He wanted to bring peace," Allonwë found herself saying slowly, remembering the archmage's words.

"What do you want from me?" Noland asked. "I can't change the past. Believe me, I've tried."

"I want you to go home, pack up your things, and leave

this country, never to return," Charlie replied. "Do not go to the land of dragons. Do not stay in here."

"Where will I go? What will I do?" Noland asked, confused why he was being sentenced like this.

"I don't really care," Charlie admitted. "But you're going to pay for what you did to the elves and dragons. You are going to lose what you find most precious: your peaceful place."

"Haven't I done my part in disappearing into the wilderness? Can't I just stay where I'm at and bother no one again?" Noland asked, desperate not to have to give up the life he had created.

"You befriended the daughter of those you slayed - those whose lives you used as weapons to harm more of her family and friends and kindred - hoping to redeem yourself. You do not deserve to disappear into the wilderness; don't deserve to redeem yourself after what you've done. Both you and your brother deserve what neither of you wanted. He wanted to live as a ruler, so he died unknown to most, a footnote in history. You want to be left alone, but you are going to be forced to travel the world and be known to all as the traitor that brought ruin to the two races of elves and dragons," Natanael spat.

"May you never be allowed to rest in peace again," Charlie said.

Noland hung his head in shame, then looked up at Charlie once more.

"For what it's worth, child," he began, but she cut him off.

"It's worth nothing coming from you," Charlie stated firmly.

"No," Allonwë said firmly, stepping forward. "You are both entitled to your opinions, and you don't have to like him or ever face him again, but I'm putting my foot down. Everyone deserves to work towards redemption. They may not see the results of it in their lifetime, but they should still be allowed to strive for it. No, what he did isn't forgivable by you," Allonwë said, looking up at Charlie. "That is your decision. But if we learned anything from Sheldane is that you can't take away someone's autonomy and still expect to be considered a decent person. Let him go to dragon capitol and offer himself up to help rebuild the relationship between elves and dragon kind."

"What?" all three of them said at the same time, looking at Allonwë with three different facial expressions that all asked the same question: Had she lost her mind?

"They'll eat me!" Noland balked.

"That's literally sending a war criminal to make amends!" Natanael argued.

"I don't want him near my kind!" Charlie declared.

"Hear me out," Allonwë said amongst their arguing. "He can tell them how he made elf and dragon magic to work in tandem to create the weapon. He can make sure that it either never happens again, or that we can build a truce and work together for the common good of the people - elf and dragon alike."

There was a long silence as the group exchanged looks between themselves at Allonwë's words.

"That... might actually be a fate worse than traveling for the rest of his days alone," Natanael reasoned, looking at Charlie and crossing her arms. "Considering that he would have to engage with dragons and elves and other people regularly in order to plan just how this spell works and recreate the compatibility between elf and dragon magic."

"I don't trust him to help my kin. What if he hurts them?" Charlie said. "Again."

"Don't count your kin out. He'll be weaponless when he goes over there with an envoy of other elves that will herald a peace treaty," Allonwë said. "We're not doing this half-heartedly."

"How will that go over?" Charlie snorted. "Here's our ambassador. By the way, he killed your leaders."

"No way! That makes you a princess too!" Allonwë

gasped. "I didn't put two and two together when he said he killed the Great Dragon and your sister was his mate!"

"I suppose it makes me a princess," Charlie reasoned. "But we use a different term in our language."

"That's amazing! You'll have to teach it to me sometime. But to answer your question, it would be more like 'We come wanting to broker a peace between our two lands. This man is responsible for this mess. We offer him to you to find out how he made the weapon that killed your leaders, and seek to work together to make sure this never happens again. We wish to make the first step in our apology by stating we have killed the man responsible for starting the Elf and Dragon wars, and this is his brother who waged them. No longer do we wish to fight, but, rather, restore the peace that we once had between our lands.' And so on and so forth." Allonwë said.

"That was really good. Did you make that up on the spot?" Natanael asked.

"Yes, someone else could probably word it better," Allonwë said. "I'm just spitballing here."

"I mean, I have some notes," Natanael said. "If you wanted to hear them."

"No," Allonwë replied.

"Okay," Natanael nodded. "But I will say this, you may not be as unprepared to make decisions as a ruler as you think you are. That was very wise of you just now."

Allonwë cut him a look, but then hesitated, shoulders going from tense to more relaxed as she thought over his words.

"You all know I'm still here, right?" Noland commented. "And that you're discussing my fate right in front of me?"

"Hush," the three others said.

"Also, Charlie, back to what I was saying before. Why didn't you tell me your sister and her mate were the king and queen of dragons?" Allonwë asked. "That means you can help with negotiations as an ambassador between your people and I can be ours!"

"I dunno," Charlie said. "Ever since my parents were killed, I've sort of just been running away from the responsibility because I don't like the idea of ruling a country. It's why my sister took over ruling in my place. I just want to hoard shiny things and spend time with my friends."

"But being a leader means you can order people to bring you shiny things when they visit you," Allonwë replied. "As a treat."

"Don't corrupt her," Natanael scolded. "That's extortion."

"It doesn't have to be money," Allonwë argued. "It can just be something shiny. Like a rock!"

"I love shiny rocks!" Charlie agreed enthusiastically.

"We're getting off topic," Natanael said flatly.

"Noland!" Allonwë declared, turning around and pointing at the elf who looked like he'd rather have been forgotten about at that point. "You have a new punishment. You are to people like you've never done so before and become a beacon of peace between our two kinds by prostrating yourself as a peace offering to the dragons."

"I wouldn't say prostrating-" Natanael began, but Allonwë shook her head.

"I said what I said. It'll take a lot to get the dragons to work with you. Prostrating is going to be the first step in getting them to hear you out because they won't expect the elf that started this all to beg for forgiveness. Or rather, not forgiveness, but atonement," she amended.

"Fair point, continue," Natanael conceded.

"Your sentencing me to death!" Noland cried.

"It's no better than you deserve," Charlie replied. "But that doesn't mean you'll get killed immediately. Dragons aren't the soulless creatures you're making them out to be. We have compassion and heart, unlike some people."

"Child, I do not doubt the heart of the dragons," Noland said. "Just their anger in the face of my crimes."

"Then you shouldn't have committed them," Charlie said simply.

"Well, I'm aware they were crimes *now*," Noland said. "But at the time, I thought I was avenging my people."

"Should've, could've, would've," Allonwë said, shaking her head and crossing her arms again. "Killing people en mass is never the answer. Defending yourself is one thing, but forming three all-out wars against the dragons? That was overkill."

"But-" Noland began.

"It has been decided," Charlie growled. "You'll be the liaison, not the ambassador."

"Who's going to be the ambassador?" Allonwë asked. "None of the ambassadors back home are going to want to do this."

"I can be the ambassador of the dragons, and you can be the ambassador of the elves until we find someone to take over in our place once we take leadership roles," Charlie replied.

"That works for me. We're the only ones brave enough to do it, I think," Allonwë said with a nod.

"Or stupid enough," Noland grumbled.

"Hey! Watch your tone," Natanael warned.

"It's okay Nana, he can be a grump for now, but when we train him to be diplomatic again, he'll learn to straighten up real fast," Allonwë said.

"Child, I was the King of Kutawë. I know how to be diplomatic," Noland argued.

"Psht," Allonwë scoffed. "Yeah, ages ago. Things have changed in the last few thousand years."

"How would you know? What are you, like twenty?" Noland scoffed back.

"I'll have you know I became of age this year! I'm forty!" Allonwë bristled.

"Gods, I'm getting old," Noland sighed. "You're still just a pup."

"I'm old enough to get married now," Allonwë replied, then let out a huge gasp. "I forgot about the engagement!"

Natanael swore under his breath. "We need to get back to Sitani castle as soon as possible. They've probably already mounted a rescue mission."

"Charlie, do you mind carrying all of us to Sitani Castle?" Allonwë asked.

"Including him?" Charlie asked wearily, nodding towards Noland.

"Yes, we have to make sure he does what we have ordered him to do and doesn't disappear into the wilderness again," Allonwë said.

"Fine," Charlie said reluctantly. "But only because I want him to see this through."

"Thank you," Allonwë said.

"Alright, everybody up," Natanael sighed.

"I ah... I can walk," Noland said.

"Noland, get on the dragon," Natanael said flatly, knowing full well he wouldn't and would try to disappear again.

"No, no, I'm good, I promise," Noland repeated.

"Old Elf, if you don't get on my back right now, I'm carrying you in my teeth this time for sure," Charlie said.

Noland finally agreed, and they all climbed on Charlie's back before she launched into the air with only a small amount of muffled screams from Natanael, who still wasn't used to flying. Allonwë let him hold on to her for dear life and relished the closeness they could have in this moment. Her heart was heavy, however, as they flew closer and closer to home.

What if she couldn't talk her parents out of this marriage? Or they tried to shoot Charlie down rather than listen? What if they put this up to her being childish again and refused to help her make peace with the dragons?

"Is that a scar on your back? Since when do you have a scar that big?" Natanael asked in her ear and Allonwë's heart sunk even further into her stomach. She hadn't told him about the fact Sheldane had carved this into her and he'd seen her in a backless dress before during ceremonies, so he knew she hadn't had one until recently.

"Let's just say I'm glad you found me when you did," Allonwë replied. "Otherwise, I wouldn't be alive right now."

There was silence from Natanael as that seemed to sink in. "I'm sorry I wasn't there sooner to stop that from happening," he said so quietly she almost couldn't hear him over the rush of wind in her ears.

But she caught it. Silently, she wrapped her arms around Natanael's arms that were holding onto her waist. It was as close as she could get to a hug at the moment as she pressed against him.

"Let's see if Charlie's magic can heal it when we finally get settled back at Sitani Castle," Natanael said. "Maybe she can do something about it. Dragon magic is very potent."

"We'll see," Allonwë nodded, then fell silent.

When Sitani castle came into view, there were bodies strewn everywhere. What looked to be a terrible battle also seemed to have ended recently. Within a few hours, by the looks of the movement within the castle. A call went up when they caught sight of Charlie racing towards them in the air. Allonwë called for her to land outside of the castle walls rather than inside them and let them see the elves riding her. That way, they would come to meet Charlie rather than Charlie going to meet them and ending with a surprise attack from the elves' side.

When they landed, the guards on the walls held bows at the ready, yelling for everyone to take aim just in case this turned into another battle. When Allonwë waved at them, calling to Colonel Mayleaf, he screamed for everyone hold fire.

"Hello Colonel Mayleaf!" Allonwë called as Natanael quickly removed his hands from her waist before anyone saw.

"Princess!" he called. "What are you doing? You went missing. Then the undead attacked. Now you're back riding a dragon? What's going on?"

"Oh, that's simple! But to prevent myself from repeating everything, do you mind getting my parents to let us in so we can all discuss this without shouting at each other?" she requested.

"Everyone? E-E-Even..." he began, glancing back at Charlie.

"Yes, especially the dragon," Allonwë nodded.

He muttered something under his breath Allonwë couldn't hear from that far away despite her elf ears and called for her to stay put. There was a solid twenty minutes of uneasy silence as they fetched her parents, the guards on the tower, hesitantly looking between her, the dragon, and each other with uncertainty in their eyes. When her mother and father appeared at the top of the wall, her mother let out a shriek.

"Allonwë! What are you doing on that dragon? Get off this instant!" she yelled.

"Hello mother!" Allonwë said as cheerfully as she could muster. She really wanted to sigh heavily and roll her eyes, but instead, she waved and smiled. This was a diplomatic mission and she couldn't show any signs of weakness to her parents or this wouldn't work. "May we land in the courtyard so we can explain everything?" she asked.

There was a silence as they processed her words, and her parents glanced at each other.

"Um," her father began. "Yes. Please do."

"Alright Charlie let's be on our best behavior," Allonwë said, mostly to herself. Charlie launched into the air, earning another shriek - this time from Allonwë's mother and not

Natanael - before she spread her wings and carefully landed in the courtyard where hundreds of eyes from the parapets and surrounding courtyard watched them closely, if not very, very nervously.

Natanael dismounted and told Noland to dismount as well, as this was Allonwë's moment in the spotlight and not theirs. He gave her the thumbs up as he noted Elias come out of the castle and spot Allonwë on Charlie's back. Elias's eyes widened. Then he looked down at Natanael, who gave him a shrug in response to his questioning expression.

"So, as you may all know, there's been a lot going on this week. First, I was forcibly betrothed to my childhood friend, which I still think is a mistake, and I'll explain why in just a moment," the princess began, looking around at the crowd and not facing her parents directly.

"Allonwë!" her mother scolded, but the princess continued on.

"But then a weapon of mass destruction went missing and turned the castle into a place of turmoil. Well, not only have I found that missing weapon, I am returning the Soul Stone inside it to the sibling of the Great Dragon that was slain to make it." Allonwë held up her wrist and removed the bracelet around her wrist. A great ruckus rose from the elves as she did this and Allonwë's parents screamed at her to stop. But she handed it to Charlie, who took it in her wing's claw.

"Thank you, Allonwë," Charlie said softly.

Allonwë gave Charlie a nod and stood up, asking if she could stand on her head. Charlie nodded, and the princess made her way up the dragon's neck, who lifted her head high for all to see.

"Now listen to me!" Allonwë yelled viciously. "All of you!" The surrounding crowd quieted down, and she continued speaking. "First, when I went after this weapon, I came across the undead. They nearly killed us for this weapon and my blood to power it to raise dragons from the dead and attack

Sitani castle. Archmage and Necromancer, Sheldane of Jeshirir, wanted to kill all of you and bring you back from the dead to create some kind of skewed world peace. But together, Charlie and I stopped him. I held him down, protected by the bracelet, and she breathed fire over him and melted him. That's what stopped the undead from attacking Sitani castle and destroying all of you. But your safety comes at a price! This bracelet is too powerful for anyone to wield as a weapon! So, we're destroying it by taking the Soul Stone out of it and giving it back to its rightful heir. Princess Charles Harold Alexander Raoul Luxembourg Ignatius the Excellent who's name I cannot pronounce in dragon yet, we're working on it, will take the stone and let her sister be reborn again in the next life."

Natanael held onto Noland by the collar of his shirt as he listened to the speech, and locked eyes with Allonwë, who remembered the next part of her speech to be one of crime and punishment.

"Second, we came across the true reason behind the elf and dragon wars. Sheldane had tricked King Noland into believing the dragons were responsible for murdering thousands of elves on our borders, but that was a lie. And Noland, believing this lie, performed many war crimes in the name of vengeance."

"What proof do you have that this is true?" someone from the crowd yelled. A rise of agreement arose. No one liking the idea that their hero was being called a war criminal.

"Noland himself!" Natanael called, pulling Noland to the forefront. He stumbled and Natanael had to right him, but the sight of his ears said this elf was old, and that he was just old enough to have been Noland's age. The crowd fell silent as Noland sighed.

"It's true," he admitted at last. "I am Noland. My brother, Sheldane, was the necromancer that lied to me and because of that lie, I started the elf and dragon wars. I didn't know he had lied until it was far too late. By the time I realized, there was no recovering from what I had done. So, I ran. I disappeared into the wilderness, never to be seen or heard from again. Until the day-" growling noises "-found me. Allonwë knows her as Charlie, But I will always know her as the individual that saved me from my spiraling madness. They can never forgive me for what I have done. But I can work for atonement for the rest of my life by becoming a liaison between the dragons and the elves to broker a peace and friendship like we once had again."

"With mine and Charlie's unbreakable friendship," Allonwë continued. "We have already started making our way towards peace. I want that for everyone in our kingdoms. No longer do I wish us to fear each other. I wish for us to be allies. So, we're going to start by offering Noland up as a peace offering to the dragons. He will teach them how he made elf and dragon magic work in tandem together so that it may never be used for evil again. After that, we will open up our borders for tentative trade again!"

A murmur ran through the crowd. They had been at war with the dragons for so long, such a statement seemed like a pipe dream. Something that seemed impossible to achieve. But here was a dragon in their midst, not harming any of them, and letting their princess stand on her head and make a speech.

"And last," Allonwë continued. "There are two things I shall decree from here on out as law. One is that Natanael shall no longer be my bodyguard, but rather the ambassador between the two lands of elves and dragons. He shall accompany me on diplomatic missions as well as attend the court ceremonies wherein we will teach him the ins and outs of how to be the best ambassador he can be. Second," she continued before Natanael could balk, as he was already trying to do just that. "A princess or prince shall, from henceforth, marry whomever they wish to marry."

"Allonwë no! Stop this instant, I won't allow this!" her mother called.

163

"No betrothals shall be had. No forced marriages shall be tolerated-" Allonwë continued only to be cut off.

There was the sound of something whizzing in the air, followed by a sharp pain embedding in her back. It knocked all the breath out of Allonwë, who took a shaky step forward onto Charlie's nose.

"Fury!" one guard yelled, followed by the sound of gurgling as his throat was slit by the fury's talons. There was a mad scramble for weapons and a call for firing at will, but all Allonwë could focus on as she tried her best to take a breath was the pain in her back. It pulsed sharply as she fell downward, tumbling endlessly until she landed in Charlie's outstretched claws.

"Allonwë!" Natanael's voice was screaming her name. Everything else was muted. Even his voice was fading from her ears.

It wasn't supposed to end like this; she thought. None of it was. She was supposed to go in, mess up, and wait for Natanael to save the day. That's all she really wanted. For him to come in and save her. Sure, it was something right out of those gag-inducing romance novels she'd once thrown across the library in disgust.

But she had just wanted something different. Something to change up the mundane world she lived in and spice things up. She didn't want to set the world ablaze; that'd been done that several times. She just wanted to escape the rules they had expected her to follow every day until she took over as ruler and eventually died of boredom.

She'd never get to tell Natanael she thought the world of him and that he sort of had become her world. That she didn't want to marry anyone, not because she thought marriage was stupid, but because if she couldn't marry her best friend, then what was the point? Sure, she and Elias were great friends. But only Natanael had been her best friend. Ever since he'd saved her from thunderstorms and taught her to love them.

She wasn't supposed to die like this. She was supposed to turn the world on its ear and Natanael was going to be there laughing with her, freely. Because she was going to make it so he could be free. That had been her plan all along. Silly Nana had always been there to protect her, even when no one was looking. Even when the things she needed protection from couldn't be seen.

And what happens?

This. This stupid thing that was never meant to be. And yet here she was, the world closing in about her, the surrounding sounds muted. The light of day fading slowly from her vision as the last thing she saw was a blazing light and Natanael's face before her. She couldn't feel the smile that crept onto her face because everything had gone numb. Couldn't feel him pick her up and cradle her as he wailed her name like a dying animal.

At least, that's how she imagined it going. She couldn't actually process anything past the pain in her back that was spreading through her chest, and leeching the life out of her. A lifetime of unrequited love finally realized in the moments of death would be something only a stupid romance novel would ever write about. But gods, what a bloody, awful ending that would be.

But what's worse?

She never got to say goodbye.

There was another blinding light that filled her vision as suddenly the air returned to her lungs. She gasped for it like a drowning sailor and she could see again. Natanael's face was the first thing she saw as he called her name, trying to get her to calm down.

"Hey, hey, I'm right here!" he said. "Breathe. Just breathe with me. You're going to be okay."

Allonwë's stomach turned decidedly ill, and she turned her face away and belched fire and bile onto the ground.

Literal fire. As if she had eaten it and was regurgitating it back up.

"Um, there may be some side effects," Charlie said hesitantly.

"To what?" Allonwë demanded sharply, wiping her mouth and looking up at her friend.

"I used my sister's Soul Stone to save you," Charlie said softly. "We almost lost you."

"A life for a life," Noland said. "Her sister's Soul Stone is now a part of you. You may notice some changes in your body."

"Like breathing fire?" Allonwë asked blatantly.

"Or growing a few scales," Noland nodded. "I've only ever heard of it happening in myths and legends, but you will take on characteristics of a dragon now that you have half the soul of one in you."

"Half the soul? What happened to the other half? And does that mean have one and a half souls now?" Allonwë asked.

"You were half dead," Noland replied. "So, Charlie replaced half of your soul with half of her sister's. That was all that was left of her sister. After all, being covered in flames and preventing one from dying from that takes a toll."

"Oh," Allonwë said, sobering. "I'm sorry Charlie... Your sister... she could have come back, but now it's my fault you'll never get to see her again."

"No," Charlie said, shaking her head. "She would have wanted me to save my friend. She would have believed in what we are doing and wouldn't want you to have died like that."

"But you'll never see her again! Why would you do that for someone you just met?" Allonwë persisted.

"Because of how far gone she was. I don't think I would have been able to see her again like she was. Not in my lifetime anyhow," Charlie said. "I'd rather her live vicariously through you than not at all."

"That's beautiful Charlie! Thank you so much... but what made you have to heal me?" the now half dragon princess asked.

"The fury apparently wasn't undead like we thought," Natanael said. "She followed us back and shot you with one of the guard's arrows. Said something about you killing the love of her life."

"Rude," Allonwë said. "And right in the middle of my speech, too."

"About what you were saying in your speech," Natanael said, helping her sit up. "Do you really have to make me an ambassador?" he groaned.

"Obviously, Nana, how else am I going to marry my best friend?" she replied.

"Wait, I thought you said you didn't want to marry Elias?" he said, confused.

"Elias isn't my best friend," Allonwë said. "You are."

The shock on Natanael's face was palpable. He opened and closed his mouth several times, trying to put his thoughts into words, but they weren't working. At length, he said, "But I'm just a bodyguard. I couldn't possibly-"

"Sure, you can. You're an ambassador now," she replied simply.

"You should marry Elias. He's been your closest friend since childhood. I've seen you two together. You would be perfect for each other."

"He's not been my best friend, you have," she repeated. "You were the one that was there for me in my darkest hours. When I feared storms, you taught me they were nothing to fear, and whenever I get lost, you always find me and save the day. I don't want to marry Elias, Nana."

"Princess..." he sighed.

"I don't hear you saying no," she countered. "I make laws now, Nana. If you tell me you don't like me like that, I'll respect your wishes, but if you tell me it's just because you don't think you're worthy, I'm going to singe your eyebrows off." When he gave her a look, she added, "I can do that now. I can breathe fire."

Natanael let out a small laugh. "I guess I've always wanted to know what it was like to marry my best friend," he admitted at last with a shy grin and Allonwë beamed, reaching out and squeezing his hand. He returned the gesture, though they both knew she would have hugged or straight up kissed him then had they not been surrounded by the courts. "But let's discuss this after you've spoken to your parents," he replied as their voices came into earshot.

Allonwë's mother was in a total state of panic as she came forward, demanding to know where her daughter was. When she found her sitting up well and healthy, she let out an exclamation before hugging her around the neck so tight Allonwë had to pat her on the shoulder to get her to ease up.

"They shot you! I saw it go straight through you! What happened?" she demanded, fretting over Allonwë.

"Mother," she said, trying to stay calm. "Meet Charlie."

Allonwë's mother looked up at the dragon, who gave her a nod.

"Charlie saved my life by sacrificing her sister's Soul Stone to keep me from dying."

"She what?" Lady Alannah breathed, glancing back up at Charlie in awe.

"How can we ever thank you?" King Kaius asked, voicing his wife's thoughts.

"Pay it forward," Charlie said. "Do not let her sacrifice be in vain. Let Allonwë and I forge an alliance between our two kinds with the help of her chosen..." Allonwë shook her head subtly where her parents couldn't see, but Charlie could, and the dragon got the gist she didn't want him to say 'fiancée' and ended the sentence with "ambassador."

Allonwë gave her a nod of thanks, breathing a sigh of relief.

The king and queen exchanged looks, then with a nod, the king left it up to his wife to decide. She stood then, brushing off her skirts, and looked around at the elves surrounding them, waiting for her decision. Taking a deep breath and letting it out slowly, Lady Alannah looked at her daughter.

"I don't know what you've gone through this past week to make you so wise in such a short time, but it must have been harrowing. Come, let us get you washed up while we get your decrees written into law."

She held out a hand to Allonwë, who smiled and took her mother's hand and getting to her feet. A great cheer went up as she stood and looked around. She was alive, and she was about to broker a peace for her people. And best of all, Natanael was going to be her ambassador.

Speaking of ambassadors...

"So, mother," she said as she fell in step with the queen and king. "About that marriage thing..."

About the Author

I. N. Knight is an emerging author of fantasy novels that take you on a fun ride from start to finish. As a fur-parent of a miniature zoo, they state if you find a typo, to blame the cats for climbing on the keyboard whilst trying avoiding the dogs. And that if you're ever in need of a laugh to join them on their Tumblr or Facebook page where you can find entertaining memes and story rantings to be shared. The QR code above takes you to their social media pages on (linktr.ee/inks.books).